REMO WAS WAITING FOR SMITH...

And he noticed immediately the small bulge in the Director of CURE's pocket. It looked like an over-stuffed envelope.

"I see you're interested in the envelope. Your tickets to Busati and your passports are in here, along with an article under your byline. You should read it. You wrote it."

"I read it," said Remo.

"It hasn't been published yet."

"Some clown who works for Lippincott showed it to me. They offered to hire me."

Smith explained Lippincott's problems. It was not just that James Forsythe Lippincott was missing in the African bush. Those things happen. CURE wouldn't bother to get involved for that, not even for a Lippincott. No, a dangerous pattern was emerging. Very dangerous. "A pattern that could undermine the American people's faith in the ability of their government to protect them," Smith said. "In the last year, several wealthy young girls from branches of the Lippincott family have met violent deaths. Or at least we thought so. But now we believe that someone is smuggling these girls out of the country to Africa, as slaves. Our sources indicate that General Obode, the President of Busati, is somehow behind this."

"Can I kill Obode?" Remo asked.

"No. But it's really a rather simple sort of operation. Get into Busati, find out wh ... ed to the missing Lipp ... out."

"You do ...

"No. But ... It's for your country ...

THE DESTROYER: SLAVE SAFARI

by
Richard Sapir & Warren Murphy

PINNACLE BOOKS • NEW YORK CITY

THE DESTROYER: SLAVE SAFARI

An original Pinnacle Books edition, published for the first time anywhere.

First printing, September 1973

Printed in the United States of America

PINNACLE BOOKS
275 Madison Avenue
New York, N.Y. 10016

For Zhana, Nina-u-penda and P. J.,
Art and Irma, and most of all for
the glorious House of Sinanju,
Box 1149, Pittsfield, Massachusetts

CHAPTER ONE

While Europe was a collection of warring tribes and Rome merely another city-state on the Tiber and the people of Israel shepherds in the Judean hills, a little girl could carry a sack of diamonds across the Loni Empire in East Africa and never fear even one being taken from her. If she suffered an injured eye, here alone in all the world were men who could repair it. In any village she could receive a parchment for her jewels, take it to any other village, then collect gems of exactly identical weight and purity. Waters from the great Busati River were stored in artificial lakes and channeled into the plains during the dry season, long before the Germanic and Celtic tribes that later became the Dutch ever heard of dikes or canals. Here alone, in all the world, a man could set his head on pillow without fear of attack in the night or hunger in the morning.

Historians do not know when the Loni ceased to care for their canals and dams, but by the time of the Arab slavers, the Loni were no more than a small tribe, hiding in the hills to escape mass slaughter. The plains were death dry; the Busati River flooded at will; and one in ten were blind for life. The land was ruled by the Hausa tribe, whose only governmental policy was to track down and to kill the remaining Loni.

Some of the Loni could not successfully hide, but instead of being killed, they were often taken to a spot on the river and traded for food and a drink called rum. Sometimes the person who took them went the way of his merchandise. Whole villages disappeared in chains to serve the plantations of the Caribbean Islands, South America and the United States. The Loni were very valuable indeed because, by this time, it had begun to be written that the men were strong and the women were beautiful and the race lacked the courage to resist.

In the year one thousand, nine hundred and fifty two, dated from the birth of a god worshipped in Europe, the Americas and small parts of Africa and Asia, the colony called Loniland became independent. In a stronger wave of nationalism in the 1960's the colony became Busati, and in a yet stronger wave in the 1970's, it expelled the Asians who had come with the British to open stores, when the lands along the Busati River had been called Loniland.

When the Asians fled under the policy called "Busatinization," the last people capable of mending an eye left the land of the Loni. Little girls dared not venture into the streets. No one carried valuables for fear of the soldiers. And high in the hills, the scattered remnants of the Loni Empire hid, waiting for a promised redeemer who would restore them to the glory that once was theirs.

CHAPTER TWO

James Forsythe Lippincott yelled for his boy who was somewhere in the Busati Hotel, which still used towels labeled Victoria Hotel and still had the ornate V's inscribed, embossed and sewn all over halls, drapes, busboys' uniforms and water faucets.

There had been no hot water since the British left, and now with the last planeload of Asians having taken off from Busati Airport the day before, there was no cold water either.

"Boy," yelled Lippincott who, back in Baltimore, would not even call a nine-year-old black child "boy." Here, he was yelling for his porter. According to the new Busati tradition, published the day before in the last edition of the *Busati Times,* any foreigner, most especially a white, who called a Busatian "boy" could be fined up to a thousand dollars, thrown in jail for ninety days and beaten with sticks.

But if you paid your fine in advance to the Minister of Public Safety and to the great conquering leader, Dada "Big Daddy" Obode, who that very morning had successfully defended Busati against an air invasion by America, Britain, Israel, Russia and South Africa, using —according to Radio Busati—the very latest in atomic planes, you would not have to pay your fine in court.

This process in Busati was called pre-guilt payment, a revolutionary system of justice.

In Baltimore the same process was called graft.

"Boy, get in here," yelled Lippincott. "There's no water."

"Yes, Bwana," came the voice from the hallway followed by a black, perspiring man in loose white shirt, loose white pants and a pair of cracked plastic shoes—which made him one of the richer men of his village ten miles up the Busati. "Walla here to serve you, Bwana."

"Get me some fucking water, nigger," said Lippincott, snapping a towel in Walla's face.

"Yes, Bwana," said Walla, scurrying from the room.

When Lippincott had come to Busati, he fully intended to respect the proud African traditions and search for old forgotten ones. But he found quickly that this politeness earned him only derision, and besides, as the Minister of Public Safety had said:

"Bush niggers need beatings, Mr. Lippincott. Not like you and me. I know it's against our laws for a white to hit a black nowadays, but between civilized men like you and me, the only way to treat a bush native is to thrash him. They're not like us Hausa. They're not even Loni, God help them. Just poor mongrels."

It was then that James Forsythe Lippincott learned of pre-guilt payments and, as he handed over two hundred-dollar bills to the Minister of Public Safety, was promised, "If any of these boys give you trouble, just let me know their names. You won't see them around anymore."

In Baltimore, James Forsythe Lippincott was careful to call the maids by their marital title and last name, and to promote blacks to executive positions in the family company he ran, but in Busati he did as the Busatians. It was the only way to get things done, he told himself, and he did not even suspect how much he truly liked this method of beatings and brutality, in preference to the enlightened Baltimore way where every problem was solved by holding another seminar in race relations.

This was Busati, and if he did not follow the Busati system of beating bush niggers, well, then, would that not be a subtle form of racism, thinking his American way was superior to the Busati way?

James Lippincott examined his stubble of a beard. He had to shave it. Couldn't let it go another day or he might be mistaken for one of the hippies who regularly never returned from Busati. In Busati, a man with a clean shave and wearing a suit got some respect. Those seeking truth, beauty and a communion with man and nature, just never showed up again.

Walla rushed into the room with a soup tureen of water.

"Why did you bring that in?" asked Lippincott.

"No more pots, Bwana."

"What happened to the pots?"

"Liberated yesterday by the army, bwana. So that imperialist aggressors won't get them. Atomic planes come to steal our pots, but our great conquering leader destroyed the attackers."

"Right," said Lippincott. "A great attack by imperialistic nations." He dipped a finger into the soup tureen of water and became angry.

"This is cold, Walla."

"Yes, Bwana, no more hot water."

"You brought up boiling water from the kitchen yesterday."

"No more gas for the stove, Bwana."

"Well, how about firewood? They can certainly burn firewood. You don't need Asians to show you how to make a fire, do you?"

"Got to go upriver for wood, Bwana."

"All right," said Lippincott, annoyed. "But for every cut I get from using cold water, you get two cuts. Understand?"

"Yes, Bwana," said Walla.

Lippincott counted three cuts on his face when he turned from the mirror and took the blade out of his safety razor.

"That's six for you, Walla."

"Bwana, I got something better for you than cutting."

"Six cuts," said Lippincott who had intentionally given himself the last two in anticipation of taking revenge for his discomfort on Walla.

"Bwana, I know where you can get woman. You need woman, Bwana, don't cut poor Walla."

"I don't want some little black ape, Walla. Now you have cuts coming to you and you know you deserve them."

"Bwana, you look. You want woman. You don't want Walla."

It was then that James Forsythe Lippincott realized his body was indeed calling out for a woman.

"White women, you do whatever you want. White women, Bwana."

"There are no white women available in Busati, Walla. That will be another cut for lying."

"White women. Oh, yes. White women. I know."

"Why haven't I heard of them before?"

"Not allowed. Not allowed. Secret. White women at the big house with the iron gate."

"A whorehouse, Walla?"

"Yes, Bwana. White women in the whorehouse. Don't cut Walla. You can do anything to them you want if you got money. Anything. You can cut white women if you got enough money."

"That's outrageous, Walla. If you're lying, I'll give you twenty cuts. Do you hear me?"

"I hear, Bwana."

When Lippincott drove up to the large white house with the iron gate, he saw to his delight that the windows held air-conditioning units. Iron bars held the gray units in place. If he had looked closer, he would have seen that there were bars also on windows that had no air conditioners. But he did not look closer, nor did he wonder why Walla did not accompany him, even though the servant knew he would be punished for just disappearing the way he had.

Lippincott was pleasantly surprised to see that the buzzer button on the gate worked. He tried it only after he found that the gate did not open to his pushing.

"Identify yourself," came a voice from a black box over the mother-of-pearl button.

"I was told I could find entertainment here."

"Identify yourself."

"I'm James Forsythe Lippincott, a close personal friend of the Minister of Public Safety."

"Then he sent you?"

If Lippincott had lived a life that exposed him to any sort of danger, he might have taken cautioned notice of the fact that in a country where brass doorknobs were stolen regularly, no one had pried loose the little mother-of-pearl buzzer from that front door. But James Lippincott was discovering himself, and in the excitement of finding that he truly loved to inflict pain, he neither worried nor cautioned.

"Yes, the Minister of Public Safety sent me and said everything would be okay," Lippincott lied. So what? Instead of a pre-guilt payment, there would be an after-guilt payment.

"All right," said the voice in the hollow raspiness of a speaker system. Lippincott could not place the accent, but it sounded faintly British.

"The car can't get through the gate," said Lippincott. "Will you send a boy out to watch it?"

"No one will touch a car in front of this gate," came the voice. The gate clicked open and such was Lippincott's anticipation that he did not wonder what might protect a car in front of this house, when ordinarily Busatians stripped a parked car like piranha working over a crippled cow.

The path to the door of the mansion was inlaid stone and the door handles shiny brass. The door of oak was polished to a gleam and the bell knob was the crafted head of a lion—not African lion but British. Lippincott knocked. The door opened and a man in Busati Army whites, with sergeant's stripes on his sleeves, stood in the entrance.

"A bit early, what?" he said in a British accent, that seemed even colder coming from his anthracite face.

"Yes. Early," said Lippincott, assuming that was what he should say.

The sergeant ushered him into a living room with ornate Victorian furniture, chairs stuffed to discomfort, bric-a-brac filling crannies, large portraits in gold frames of African chiefs. It was not British, but almost British. Not the almost-British of Busati, but the almost-British of another colony. Lippincott could not place it.

The sergeant motioned Lippincott to a seat and clapped his hands.

"A drink?" he said, lowering himself into a stuffed sofa.

"No, no, thank you. We can begin now," he said.

"You must have a drink first and relax," said the sergeant, grinning. An old wizened black woman came into the room silently.

"We'll have two of your special mint juleps," the sergeant said.

Mint juleps. That was it. This home was furnished the pre-Civil War South, *American South,* thought Lippincott. Like a pre-Civil War whorehouse, perhaps in Charleston, South Carolina.

Lippincott made a show of looking at his watch.

"Don't rush yourself, the girls will wait," said the sergeant. The man was exasperating, thought Lippincott.

"Tell me, Lippincott, what brings you to Busati?"

Lippincott resented the over-familiar use of the last name, but answered, "I'm an amateur archaeologist. I'm looking for the causes of the breakdown of the great Loni Empire and the assumption of power by the Hausa tribe. Look. I'm not really thirsty and I'd like to get on with, well, with the business at hand."

"I'm sorry for the inconvenience," said the sergeant, "but you are not on the approved list to use this house, so I'll have to find out more about you before you may begin. Terribly sorry, old boy."

"All right, what do you want to know?"

"Must you make it seem like an interrogation, old boy?" the sergeant said. "Interrogations are so crass."

"When crass is faster, crass is nicer."

"All right, if you must be barbaric, who told you of this place?"

"The Minister of Public Safety," lied Lippincott.

"Did he tell you the rules?"

"No."

"The rules are these. You don't ask the girls their names. You tell no one of this house. No one. And, old boy, you don't just drive up to the gate. You phone in advance. Make an appointment. Understand?"

"Yeah. Yeah. C'mon. How much?"

"It depends upon what you want to do."

Lippincott did not feel comfortable talking about it. He had never done this before, not what he wanted to do, and before coming to Busati had never even suspected that he had such desires. He fumbled with the words, stepping into the area of his longings, then skirting them, then approaching them from another angle.

"Whips and chains, you mean," said the sergeant.

Lippincott nodded silently.

"That's not so unusual. Two hundred dollars. If you kill her, that's $12,000. Severe damage is prorated. These girls are valuable."

"All right, all right. Where do I go?"

"Cash in advance."

Lippincott paid, and after insolently recounting the money, the sergeant led him upstairs to a long broad hallway. They stopped in front of a polished steel door. From a tall chest next to the door, the sergeant took a cardboard box, and handed it to Lippincott.

"Your whips and chains are in here. Hooks are on

the wall. If the girl gives you any trouble, just ring the buzzer in the room. If she refuses you anything, threaten to ring the buzzer. She shouldn't be any trouble though. Been here three months. Only the really new ones give trouble. Haven't been educated, so to speak."

The sergeant took a key from a ring on his belt and unlocked the door. Lippincott gripped the paper box tightly under his arm and went into the room like a schoolboy discovering an abandoned pastry shop.

He slammed the door behind him, and in his rush into the room, almost stumbled over a wide metal cot. On it lay a nude woman, her legs drawn up to her stomach, her arms shielding her head, her red hair a dirty tangle on the mattress, which was speckled with dried bloodstains.

The room smelled of camphor and Lippincott assumed it must be from the ointment that glistened on the girl's flanks over fresh and precisely drawn lash marks. Lippincott suddenly felt compassion for the creature and was tempted to leave the room, perhaps even buy her freedom, when she peered from beneath her folded arms and seeing a man with a box, rose slowly from the cot. When he saw her young breasts flecked with dried blood as she rose from the cot, a driving rage enveloped him, and when she dutifully walked to the dirty, blood-spattered wall and raised her hands above her head to an iron ring, Lippincott was trembling. He fumbled the chains around her wrists, then pounced on the whip as if someone might snatch it from him.

As he readied himself for the stroke, the girl asked, "Do you want screaming?" She was American.

"Yes, screaming. Lot of screaming. If you don't scream, I'll whip harder and harder."

Lippincott whipped and the girl screamed with each cutting crack. Back came the whip, then forward, crack, and the polished snakelike cord glistened with blood, back and forward, back and forward, faster until the screams and the whip and the cracking became a single sound of anguish and then it was over. James Forsythe Lippincott was spent and with the sudden quenching of his strange and sudden thirst, his powers of reasoning assumed command and he was suddenly afraid.

He realized now the girl had screamed almost as a duty despite the great pain. She was probably drugged. Her back looked like raw meat.

What if someone had taken pictures of him? He could deny them. It would be his word against some bush nigger's. What if the Minister of Public Safety found out he used his name improperly? Well, three, maybe four hundred dollars would take care of that.

What if the girl died? Twelve thousand dollars. He gave more than that each year to the Brotherhood Union for Human Dignity.

So why be afraid?

"Are you through, Lippy?" the redheaded girl asked dully, her voice heavy with drugs. "If you are, you're supposed to take the chains off."

"How do you know my name? That's only used in my social circle."

"Lippy, this is Busati. Are you through?"

"Uh, yes," he said, going to the wall to get a better look at her face in the dimly lit room. She was about twenty five, the fine, lean nose had been broken days before and was swollen and blue now. There was a gash in the lower lip that had crusted around the edges.

"Who are you?"

"Don't ask. Just let me die, Lippy. We're all going to be dead."

"I know you, don't I? You're . . . you're," and he saw the features, now mangled, that had once graced Chesapeake Bay society, one of the Forsythe girls, a second cousin.

"What are you doing here, Cynthia?" he said, and then, in horror, remembered and said, "We just buried you in Baltimore."

"Save yourself, Lippy," she groaned.

In his panic, that was just what Lippincott intended to do. He envisioned Cynthia Forsythe somehow getting back to Baltimore and disclosing his terrible secret. Lippincott grabbed the end of the whip and wrapped it around the girl's neck.

"You're a fool, Lippy, you always were," she said and James Forsythe Lippincott tightened the whip and kept pulling the ends until the red swollen face of the girl disclosed a tongue and the eyes bulged and he kept pulling.

The sergeant downstairs understood why James Forsythe Lippincott did not wish to write out a personal check, and yes, he would trust him to return to his hotel and make arrangements with the National Bank of Busati to get cash. "We do not worry," the sergeant said. "Where would you go?"

Lippincott nodded, although he was not sure what the sergeant meant. He understood only that he would be allowed to pay for what happened upstairs, and that was all he wanted to hear.

When Lippincott returned to his hotel, Walla was still missing. He called for him several times, then vowed that when he saw Walla again, the busboy would get a beating to carry on his back for the rest of his life.

The vice-president of the bank offered to supply guards to Lippincott because walking around Busati with $12,000 was not the wisest of courses. "This is not New York City," the banker explained, apologetically and inaccurately.

Lippincott refused. He was sorry three blocks later. One of the many military patrols stopped him and as he reached into his pocket to show his identification and a ten-dollar bill, he must have disclosed the bulk of his cash, for the officer reached into his pocket and took out the envelope of one hundred and twenty hundred-dollar bills.

"That belongs to the house with the iron gate," said Lippincott hoping the power the house seemed to have would extend to the officer. Apparently it didn't, because the officer simply double-checked Lippincott's identification, asked him again if he were indeed James Forsythe Lippincott, then shoved him into the Land Rover and personally drove the vehicle away.

Out of the capital they drove, and along the great Busati River they drove. Darkness fell over the Busati and still they drove on, alone, the rest of the patrol having been ordered to stay back in the city. They drove so far that when they stopped Lippincott swore the stars seemed close, as close and as clear as they must have been when man first descended from the trees.

The officer told Lippincott to get out.

"Look, I can give you twice that amount of money. You don't have to kill me," said Lippincott.

"Get out," said the officer.

"I'm a personal friend of the Minister of Public Safety," said Lippincott.

"You'll find him over there behind that wide tree," said the officer. "Go."

So Lippincott, finding the Africa night chilly and his heart even chillier, went to the wide tree that rose like a little prickly mountain from the Busati plain.

"Hello?" he said but no one answered. His elbow brushed up against something on the tree. He looked around. It was a boot. A leg was in the boot and on top of the leg was a body. The dangling hands were black. The body did not move and it smelled of the last release of the bowels. The body was in an officer's uniform. Lippincott stepped back to escape the smell and to try for a better look at the face. Suddenly a flashlight illuminated the body's features. It was the Minister of Public Safety. A large spike protruded from his head. He had been nailed to the tree.

"Hello, Lippy," said an American voice.

"What?" gasped Lippincott.

"Hello, Lippy. Squat down on your haunches. No, not your butt on the ground. On your haunches, like a slave waiting for his master. On the haunches. That's right. Now, Lippy, before you die, if you're very nice, you may ask me a question."

The flashlight had gone off and now the voice came out of the African dark, and try as he might, Lippincott could not see the speaker.

"Look," he said, "I don't know who you are, but I can make you a rich man. Congratulations on successfully scaring the crap out of me, Now, how much?"

"I've got what I want, Lippy."

"Who are you?"

"Is that your one question?"

"No, my one question is what do you want?"

"All right, Lippy, I'll answer that. I want to revenge my people. I want to be accepted in my father's house."

"I'll buy your father's house. How much?"

"Ah, Lippy, Lippy, Lippy. You poor fool."

"Look. I want to live," said Lippincott, straining to keep his backside just off his raised heels. "I'm humbling myself. Now what can I give you for my life?"

"Nothing. And I don't care about your humbling yourself. I'm not some Harlem shine who calls himself Abdulla Bulbul Amir. Humbling doesn't do anybody any good."

"You're white? I can't see."

"I'm black, Lippy. African. Does that surprise you?"

"No. Some of the most brilliant men in the world are black."

"If you had any chance at all, you just blew it with that lie," the voice said. "I know better. I know every one of you Lippincotts and Forsythes. There isn't one of you who isn't a racist."

"What do you want?" asked Lippincott. "What do you want?" The man was obviously keeping him alive for something. There was silence. Far off, a hyena howled. There would be no lions near here, not with vehicles and men having been around the area.

"I can get you recognition from America," said Lippincott. "My family can do that."

"Who is America to recognize or not to recognize?"

"What do you want?"

"Some information."

"If you kill me, you won't get it."

"First I'll get it and then I'll kill you. There are many ways to die and some aren't so bad."

Lippincott believed the man and like many people who find death too strong to face, he told himself a little lie. He told himself he would be spared if he told the man the truth.

"The Minister of Public Safety didn't tell you about the house, did he?"

"No, he didn't," Lippincott said, remembering again the gruesome corpse hanging from the tree near his head. "My boy Walla did."

"Never mind, the Minister had to die anyway," the voice said. "Unlike most members of this government, he would not see things my way. Now, you've done research on slave ships and the original slave trade into the States. There was a Butler plantation on which you still have the records, isn't that so?"

"Yes. I can show them to you. They're at my Chesapeake Bay estate."

"In the basement storage or the library?"

"I forget. But I can show you."

"No matter. We'll get them, now that we know which of your homes they're in. That's all I needed. Anything I can give you besides your life?"

"Nothing," said Lippincott on the hope that if only his life would do for a favor, his life he might get.

"Don't you want to know the answer to your research about the breakup of the great Loni Empire?"

"I want my life."

The voice ignored him. "The Loni Empire," it said, "broke up because it put its faith in outsiders. It hired people to do what it should have done itself. And they grew soft and weak, and finally the Hausa just pushed them over, as if they were soft, fat children."

Despite his predicament, Lippincott was interested. "That's too simple," he said. "To build a great empire takes character. The Loni must have had it. They would not just roll over and play dead."

"No, you're right," the voice said. "They would have fought. But something got in the way. Your family's accursed slave trade. So the best of the Loni wound up shipped away to grow cotton for you. But I'll tell you a story. The Loni are going to return to power again. I hope that makes you feel better."

"It doesn't," Lippincott said, "but suppose you tell me how. Right now, the whole Loni tribe couldn't build a shoebox."

"Simple," the voice said. "I'm going to lead them back to power." He paused. "Really horrible thing you did to that girl. Not that it matters, Lippy. Not that she matters or that you matter. You'd have to pay a long time before the Lippincotts and the Forsythes ever got even. It doesn't matter. What matters is in the mountains."

Lippincott heard the hyena sounds and smelled the death smells of the Minister of Public Safety and felt a sudden great shock to his back, that came out his chest, and he fell forward on a spear that was through his body. When his head hit the Busati plain, he was dead, another small piece of fertilization, no more than an ancient Loni emperor or an ancient Loni child. Africa took him as one of its own, the earth as ever being the only truly equal opportunity employer in the history of man.

Walla, being more intelligent than either the Minister of Public Safety or Lippincott, was safely up the Busati River in his village. He had something to sell of far greater value than the last pieces of silver engraved with the old English "V" at the Busati Hotel. He had information; information was always salable.

Hadn't the clerk from the Ministry of Justice sold a copy of the files of the Busati secret police for gold—real gold—coins you could roll in your hands and buy fifty wives with or twenty cattle or shoes and plows and shirts and maybe even a radio for private use, instead of sharing it with the whole village?

So Walla told his brothers he was leaving the village and that his eldest brother should meet him over the border in Lagos, Nigeria in a month.

"You are selling tales, Walla?" asked the elder brother.

"It is best you do not know what I do," said Walla wisely. "Governments do terrible things to people who know things."

"I have often wondered why we have governments. Tribal chiefs never did terrible things to people who knew things."

"It is the white man's way."

"If the white man is not here anymore, and if, as the radio says, we are getting rid of everything white, why cannot we get rid of white governments?"

"Because the Hausa downriver are fools," Walla said. "They want to get rid of the white man so they can *be* white men."

"The Hausa have always been fools," said the elder brother.

In jeeps with massive supplies, the journey to Lagos would have taken a Busati army patrol a month. Walla, carrying a knife and no food, made the journey on foot in sixteen days.

Walla found a neighbor from his village and asked him for a good place to sell information.

"Not here," said the neighbor who was an assistant gardener at the Russian Embassy. "They were paying good last year but this year is terrible. The Americans are best again."

"The Chinese, are they good?" asked Walla.

"Sometimes they are good, but often they think it is enough to tell you funny stories in exchange for your information."

Walla nodded his head. He had heard these things of the yellow men back in Busati, how they would give a button or a book and think of that as payment, and then be surprised and angry when told that was not nearly enough.

"Americans are the best again," said the gardener, "but take only gold. Their paper is worth less each day."

"I will take gold and I will return here and see you. Your information has been of value."

"See the cook at the American Embassy. He will tell you the price to ask."

The cook at the American Embassy promptly fed Walla and listened to his story, asking questions so that Walla would be well-prepared to negotiate.

"This Lippincott disappearing is a good thing. Quite valuable. But the nature of the house is even more valuable possibly. Who are these white women?"

Walla shrugged. "I do not know."

"Who frequents the house?" the cook asked.

"I was told of it by a soldier. He said that Busati soldiers who do good things are given leave to go to the house and do terrible things to the women."

"Does President Obode run the house?" the cook asked.

"I do not know. I think not. I was told that the sergeant who is at the house is a Loni."

"A Loni? Are you sure he is not a Hausa? Hausa do those sort of things."

"I know Hausa from Loni," said Walla. "He is a Loni."

"A Loni who is a sergeant. That is very important," the cook said.

"It is worth gold?" Walla asked.

The cook shook his head. "The Americans do not know Loni from Hausa and could not care less that a Loni has reached a sergeant's rank in Busati's army. Do you have anything on the women in the house?"

"They never come out alive."

The cook shrugged a so-what shrug.

"I know a name. It was told to me by a fellow of our village who worked at the airport. I remember it because it was like Lippincott's name."

"Her name was Lippincott?" the cook asked.

"No. Forsythe. Lippincott had a Forsythe in his name. My friend said he saw her being taken from a plane to a car. She screamed who she was, and then was dragged into the car. She said she was Cynthia Forsythe of Baltimore."

"What did she look like?"

"White," Walla said.

"Yes, but what kind of white? All whites do not look alike."

"I know that," said Walla. "Our friend said she had hair of flame."

The cook thought about this and did not respond immediately. Instead he began chopping vegetables for dinner. When he had finished shredding long green leaves, he snapped his fingers.

"Eighteen thousand dollars. Gold," he said.

"Eighteen thousand dollars?" asked Walla, astounded.

The cook nodded. "That is what we ask for. We settle for fifteen." And he told Walla to withhold the name of the girl until he got the money, but to mention Lippincott's name quickly to make sure he got the money. He explained that the man he would introduce Walla to was J. Gordon Dalton, who was some kind of a spy. He would offer Walla ten dollars or twenty dollars, whereupon Walla should get up to leave, and then Dalton would pay the fifteen thousand.

"I knew a man who had a hundred dollars once," said Walla. "A very rich man."

"You will be rich too," said the cook.

"I will have to be. I can no longer return to Busati."

By nightfall, Walla was the richest man in the history of his village and J. Gordon Dalton was sending frantic codes to Washington. A top level officer unscrambled the message:

JAMES FORSYTHE LIPPINCOTT, BALTIMORE, MISSING. BELIEVED DEAD IN BUSATI BUSH. FOUL PLAY SUSPECTED. CYNTHIA FORSYTHE, BALTIMORE, HELD HOSTAGE. AWAIT INSTRUCTIONS. INVESTIGATING.

Since Lippincott was part of the famous Lippincott family which numbered governors, diplomats, senators and most important, bankers, the message went to several department heads at 4:00 A.M. There was one problem with Dalton's message. Cynthia Forsythe could not be a hostage in Busati. She had been killed in an auto accident three months earlier. It had made the papers because she was related to the Lippincotts.

It was decided quietly to check out the dead girl's body. By noon, from dental work and a thumb print, the body was identified as not, *definitely not,* the body of Cynthia Forsythe.

"Who is it then?" asked the State Department man.

"Who cares?" said the FBI man. "It's not the Forsythe girl. That means she probably *is* a hostage in Busati."

"Well, we're going to have to tell the White House," said State. "God help anyone who runs afoul of the Lippincotts. Especially the bankers."

Five reports on the case were made in the White House, four of which went to various Lippincotts. The fifth was hand-delivered to an office in the Agriculture Department in Washington, where it was coded and sent by scrambler to what the sender believed was an office in Kansas City. But the line went to a sanitarium in Rye, New York, and in that sanitarium a decision was made that unknowingly fulfilled an ancient prediction made soon after the Loni tribe had lost its empire:

"Terror from the East shall join with terror from the West, and woe to the enslavers of the Loni when the destroyer of worlds walks along the Busati."

CHAPTER THREE

His name was Remo and his life was being made miserable by a television programming decision.

"Because of our coverage of the Senate investigation into Watergate, *As the Planet Revolves* and *Dr. Lawrence Walters, Psychiatrist-at-Large* will not be shown today," the announcer had said.

When Remo heard that, he uttered his first prayer since childhood. "Lord, have mercy on us all."

The wisp of an Oriental who had sat placid in his golden kimono before the color television set, let out a sound Remo had heard him use but once before, and then only in his sleep.

"Yaaawk," said Chiun, the Master of Sinanju, his wisp of a white beard shaking in disbelief. It was if someone had hit the old man a body blow—that is, if there was a man who walked the earth who could do that, which Remo doubted very much.

"Why is this? Why is this?" demanded Chiun.

"Not me, Little Father. Not me. I didn't do it."

"Your government did it."

"No, no. The television people did it. They thought that more people would want to watch the Senate investigation than the soap operas."

Chiun pointed a long bony finger at the set. The long fingernail seemed to quiver.

"Who would want to watch those ugly white men when they can see the beauty and the rhythm and the grace of true drama?"

"Well, they have polls, Chiun. And they question people about what they like and don't like and I guess they figured more people would want to watch the investigations than your serials."

"They did not ask me," said Chiun. "No one asked me. Who asked me? If they asked me, I would say let the beauty of the drama remain. Beauty is rare but investigations you have with you always. Where is this person who does the questioning? I would speak with him for surely he would be interested in my opinion also."

"You're not going to kill a pollster, Little Father," said Remo.

"Kill?" said Chiun, as if Remo had broached the subject to a Carmelite nun, instead of the most deadly assassin in existence.

"Those things do tend to happen, Chiun, when someone gets in the way of your daytime shows. Or are you forgetting Washington and those FBI men, or New York and all those Mafiosi? You remember. They turned off your programs. Chicago and the union thugs. Remember? Remember who had to get rid of the bodies? Do you forget those little things, Little Father?"

"I remember beauty being interrupted and an old man, who has given the best years of all his skills to an ingrate, being reprimanded for attempting to enjoy a moment of beauty."

"You have a very selective memory."

"In a country that fails to appreciate beauty, a memory which forgets ugliness is a necessity."

And that had begun the renewed personal supervision of Remo's training by the Master of Sinanju. No longer could Remo do his exercises alone. Deprived of his daytime TV shows, Chiun had to supervise the basics and Remo could do nothing right.

Sitting by Lake Patusick in the Massachusetts Berkshires where they rented a cottage for the spring, Remo heard Chiun tell him he breathed like a wrestler. During the water movements, Chiun screamed that Remo moved like a duck, and when Remo was doing the stomach flips—an exercise in which Remo lay flat on his stomach and then used his abdominal muscles to flip himself over onto his back—Chiun said Remo moved like a baby. "You should have a nurse, not the Master of Sinanju. That was slow and clumsy."

Remo assumed the position again, the spring grass near the cool Berkshire lake tickling his cheeks, the smell of the fresh muddy rebirth of life in his nostrils, the morning sun on his bare back, illuminating but not warming. He waited for Chiun's click of fingers to signal the flip. It was a simple exercise, trained into his reflexes more than a decade before, as he began the training that changed a man the public thought had been electrocuted into the killer arm of a secret organization that was designed to fight crime.

Remo waited for the snap of the fingers but it did not come. Chiun was having him wait. Better to wait, he thought, than have to find a place to put the body of the man who was responsible for taking *As the Planet Revolves* off the air. He felt a slight pressure on his back, probably a leaf falling.

He heard the snap of Chiun's fingers and his stomach muscles slapped the ground like springs released from restraint, but his body did not spin around as Remo expected. The instant pressure of two feet on his back sent his body flat down in the wet spring mud. Remo spit the mud out of his mouth. It was not a leaf he had felt fall on his back, but the Master of Sinanju alighting, weightlessly on him. Remo heard the chuckles above him.

"Do you need help, little baby?"

To the untrained eye, it would appear that a thirtish man of moderate build with extra thick wrists and dark hair had attempted a pushup and failed because an old Oriental was standing on his back. Actually, the force expended by both men could shatter slate.

This simple little accident was viewed by three men who had walked around from the front of the cottage and now stood watching the pair—the young white man face in mud, the aged Oriental giggling.

The three men wore dark business suits. The shortest carried a briefcase, the others .25 caliber Berettas that they believed were hidden under their jackets.

"I'm looking for a Remo Mueller," said the man with the briefcase. Remo lifted his head from the mud and felt Chiun alight from his back. He wanted to send a razor sharp hand into the old man's giggling face, but he knew the cutting edge of the hand would be jelly before it ever touched the face. Perhaps in ten years, his mind and body would equal Chiun's and then maybe Chiun would not use Remo as a punching bag for his frustrations.

Remo saw by the way the two taller men stood that they were carrying weapons. There is a reaction of the body to a weapon it carries, a certain heaviness of the body around the weapon. The two men stood with heaviness.

"Remo Mueller?" asked the man with the briefcase.

"Yes. That's me," said Remo, spitting out mud. He had been given the name Mueller several weeks before. This was the first time he'd heard anyone use it, and he wondered if it should be pronounced Muell-er as in fuel, or Muell-er as in full. This man pronounced it as in full.

"The name's pronounced Mueller . . . as in fuel," Remo said, deciding that Chiun had no corner on perversity this day.

"I'd like to talk to you about a magazine article you wrote for the *National Forum of Human Relations.*"

Magazine article. Magazine article, thought Remo. Sometimes upstairs planted an article under his byline when they wanted to give him a cover as a magazine reporter, but he did not remember being informed of any article by upstairs recently. He had been told to rest.

Remo stared blankly at the man. What could he say? "Let me see the article I was supposed to have written." Upstairs moved in peculiar ways, right from the first day when former Newark policeman Remo Williams discovered that upstairs had been responsible for the frameup that put him in the electric chair, and equally responsible for getting him out alive, the man who did not exist for the agency which did not exist.

The explanation was simple, as most of upstairs' explanations were. The Constitution no longer worked; the country could no longer withstand the onslaught of crime. The answer was an organization that functioned outside the Constitution, doing whatever it had to do to equalize the odds.

"And I'm the guy who's going to do the dirty work?" Remo had asked.

"You're elected," he was told. Thus began a decade of training under Chiun, the Master of Sinanju, a decade in which Remo had lost count of the number of people he had killed, just remembered the moves.

"Would you care to talk inside?" Remo asked the three men.

The gentlemen said they would be happy to do so.

"Ask them if they know the vile pollsters of Washington," said Chiun.

"I think this is business," said Remo, hoping that Chiun would choose to get lost. Only three men knew that the secret crime-fighting organization called CURE existed, and Chiun was not one of them. But as the Master of Sinanju, there was only one thing he needed to know of an employer. Did he pay on time and did his payments reach Sinanju, the little Korean village that Chiun and his ancestors had supported through the centuries by renting out their deadly assassin's skills? This question being answered affirmatively, Chiun would not have cared if his employer were the Girl Scouts of America.

"Business, business, business," said Chiun. "You are a nation of businessmen."

"Your servant?" asked the man with the briefcase.

"Not exactly," said Remo.

"Do you men know the vile pollsters of Washington?" asked Chiun.

"We might," said the man with the briefcase.

"Chiun, I think this is work. Please," said Remo.

"We can be of help in many ways," said the man with the briefcase.

"He doesn't need your help. Inside if you please," said Remo, but Chiun, hearing that there might be some way of restoring his daytime soap operas to the screen, followed the gathering into the cottage. He sat cross-legged on the floor watching the men on couches and chairs.

"This is confidential," said the man with the brief-case. He had the quiet authority of one backed by much wealth.

"Ignore him," Remo said of Chiun.

"Your magazine article proved of great interest to my employer. I saw your surprise when I mentioned it. I can understand your wondering how we saw the article when it won't even be published until next week."

Remo nodded as if he knew what the article was about.

"I have a question for you," the man said. "Just what are your contacts with Busati?"

"I'm afraid that all my sources are confidential," said Remo who did not know who or what or where a Busati was.

"I admire your integrity. Mr. Mueller, let me be frank. We might want you for something."

"Like what?" asked Remo, noticing the edge of a manuscript poke from the man's briefcase.

"We'd like to hire you as a consultant for our offices in Busati."

"Is that my story you have in there?" Remo said.

"Yes. I wanted to discuss it with you."

Remo reached out a hand for the manuscript. "Just want to review it myself," he said.

Even under an assumed name, Remo felt embarrassed by the story. Busati, he quickly surmised, was a country. According to what he was supposed to have written, Busati was forging new forms of socialism after throwing off colonialist chains, under the guidance of President General Dada "Big Daddy" Obode. Any report of tribal friction was an invention of the neo-colonialistic fascist imperialistic powers who feared the enlightened progressive leadership of the Saviour of Busati, General Obode, who brought electricity to the villages, ended crime in the capital and had made the first major inroads against poverty in Busati since the white man had first enslaved the little nation. Why this capitalist fear of Obode? Because his brilliance threatened to undermine the substructure of racist oppressive Western government and all Western nations quaked before the glory of his brilliance.

The article was called "An Unbiased View of Busati." Remo returned the manuscript.

"You're rather an interesting fellow, Mr. Mueller," the man said. "We looked into your background and, frankly, we found nothing at all. Not a thing. Not even fingerprints. Now a traveler of your stature should have prints in someone's file. Do you mind telling us why not."

"Yes," said Remo. He turned to Chiun. "What's for dinner?"

"I have not decided," said Chiun.

"Of course, your background is your business," said the man with the briefcase. "We just wish to employ you at great profit to yourself. Very great."

"Duck would be good," said Remo, "if you cooked it right."

"We had duck last night," said Chiun.

"I'm here to make you an offer you can't refuse,"

said the man with the briefcase, smiling a wide row of very even white teeth.

"What?" said Remo.

"An offer you can't refuse."

"I'm refusing it," said Remo.

"Can you refuse $2,000 a week?"

"Sure," said Remo.

"Are you willing to see your stories turned down by every magazine in the country? It would not be hard for you to get a reputation as an unreliable nut, and then who would print your stories?"

"Who cares?" Remo said. He thought of the article he was supposed to have written. If that was sanity, he wondered what magazines thought insanity was.

"Come now, Mr. Mueller. I represent the Lippincott Foundation. Surely you've heard of us. A year's contract with us for one hundred thousand dollars could *make* an ambitious young man like you. You'd have the Lippincott family behind you forever."

Remo looked at the man and thought deeply for a moment.

"So what's wrong with duck two days in a row?" he asked Chiun.

"Nothing is wrong with duck two days in a row. There is just nothing very right with it two days in a row," said Chiun.

"Mr. Mueller, I'm talking to you."

"I know," said Remo. "Why don't you stop?"

"Mr. Mueller, if that's who you are, we have vital interests in Busati. We want only an introduction to the leadership of that country. We cannot use formal diplomatic channels because all whites and Asians have been expelled from the country. Just an introduction, that's all we want from you. It might take you only a day, or just a few hours. For that, you would be a wealthy man. For not doing that, you will be a ruined man. Now what is your answer?"

"Right or wrong, duck," said Remo.

"I'm sorry it has to be this way, Mr. Mueller. I'm going outside. I will be back in five minutes or whenever I hear the word 'yes' yelled at the top of your lungs. If you still have lungs."

The man with the briefcase rose somberly and walked to the front door. He left it open and Remo could see him light a cigarette in the front yard. The two men with the concealed weapons rose and approached Remo.

"Stay out of this, old man, and you won't be hurt," one said to Chiun. The Master of Sinanju smiled sweetly. "Oh, thank you so much for sparing a frail old man."

Remo shot him a dirty look. He didn't like it like this, not with Chiun watching. There would be non-stop bitching later on about Remo's technique. Well, Remo would be very simple and stick to basics. He was not in the mood for a harangue.

"We would rather be easy on you," said the man nearest Remo. He grabbed Remo's wrist and twisted ever so slightly. It was a move of either kung fu or karate, but Remo did not remember. Chiun liked to catalog these foolishnesses, but Remo did not want to be bothered. All of them were incomplete tools, even at their most advanced levels where they became workable for actual use. This man was being "the clinging vine" or something. He twisted.

Remo saw Chiun watch his elbow. Damn. Well, whatever. Remo brought his gripped hand back, taking the man with him and caught the chestbone with his right thumb. A single timed move that enabled him to step over the falling breathless body to the man facing Chiun, who now realized what Remo was doing. Remo tried to put the second man between him and Chiun so that Chiun would not witness the stroke.

The man guarding the old Oriental saw his parchment bearded face, saw him suddenly dart into a crouching position and look around the man's waist. The man looked down behind him, but saw nothing. Suddenly everything was black.

"Your stroke was rushed on the second man. I could not see the first because of the falling body," Chiun said.

"You couldn't see the second either, Little Father."

"I saw it."

"You cannot see through flesh."

"I saw the stroke of your hand in the heel of that foot," said, Chiun, pointing to the man on the floor. "It was rushed."

One of the men twitched.

"Well, the stroke worked," Remo said glumly.

"A child playing by the beach builds castles that work also, but they are not enough to live in and certainly not enough for the storm. You must build a house for the storm, not for the sunny afternoon. Your stroke was for a sunny afternoon."

"These guys were a sunny afternoon."

"I cannot reason with you," said Chiun and lapsed into a stream of Korean with such recognizable terms—to Remo—as the inability of even the Master of Sinanju to make a banquet from rice husks or diamonds from mud.

The man with the briefcase returned to the cottage with an order: "Don't you two guys hurt him too much.

We need him," he said and then he saw his two guys.

"Oh," he said.

"They faw down, go boom," Remo said. "Now I'd like to ask you a question or two in all fairness and honesty."

To assure fairness and honesty, Remo placed a hand very quickly on the back of the man's neck, and as he pinched a nerve just so, the man too felt fairness and honestly were the only way to answer questions.

He worked for the Lippincott Foundation. His direct boss was Laurence Butler Lippincott. Another Lippincott, James Forsythe, had disappeared in the Busati bush. The government was working on it, but Laurence Butler Lippincott thought he could do better. Remo Mueller was wanted because he obviously was friends with General Obode. The Lippincotts would use him to get to Obode, to get his help in finding James Forsythe Lippincott. Laurence Lippincott himself had ordered that Remo be approached.

Remo released the pinch on the nerve.

"Your friends will come to in a moment or so," he said. "Where I can find Laurence Butler Lilliput?"

"Lippincott," the man said. "No one finds Mr. Lippincott. You see him by appointment only, if you're lucky."

Remo decided to rephrase the question and there must have been something in the manner of his voice because he got an immediate response. Laurence Butler Lippincott was at the headquarters of the International Bank of New York City, 88th floor, the Lippincott Suite.

He appeared promptly each morning at 11:30 A.M. and worked through till 4:30 P.M. Non-stop. He was the responsible Lippincott. Remo released the man's neck again.

"No one gives Mr. Lippincott orders," said the briefcase man. "Maybe you stopped me, but there'll be more. No one can stand up against vast money. No one. Not governments. Not you. No one. All you can do is serve and hope you'll be rewarded."

"You will personally see your vast money in little soggy lumps," Remo said.

"Have you learned nothing?" shrieked Chiun. "Boasting? A boast is more fatal than a rushed stroke. A boast is a gift to an enemy. Have you learned nothing?"

"We'll see," said Remo. "Do you want to come along?"

"No," said Chiun. "A boast is bad enough but a successful boast is worse because it encourages other boasts, and they surely will cost in price. Nothing in this world is without payment."

Payment was a good word and Remo thought about it as the briefcase man drove him to New York City. Every so often, the two bodyguards would wake up and Remo would put them back to sleep. This went on until the Taconic Parkway when the two men finally got the general idea that they were no longer expected to overpower Remo.

Laurence Butler Lippincott did not have his offices in the huge tower his banks were famous for financing. They were instead in a tall, aluminum, looming building just off Wall Street, a narrow side street made wider by a large open entranceway with modern sculpture, which the briefcase man told Remo cost the Lippincotts more than two million in lost office space. Most people were amazed that Lippincott had spent $70,000 for the sculpture, but never considered that it cost so much more just to give it space. If Remo would think about reality, he too would appreciate what working for Lippincott meant. Remo did not appreciate reality.

He pushed the two bodyguards and the briefcase man ahead of him and managed to compress them all in a revolving door with the breaking of only one bone, the briefcase man's left arm which didn't quite fit. He screamed appropriately.

They had to take two elevators to the Lippincott floor. The first went only up to the 60th floor where three guards and a manager questioned Remo and his party.

Remo was polite and he was honest. He told the three guards and the manager that he was going to see Mr. Lippincott and would be delighted if they would accompany him. This, three of them did, with happy hearts. They were happy because they were not the fourth man who lay on the carpeting of the sixtieth floor foyer with his ribs and nose broken. The happy throng burst out into the 88th floor with exuberance, two guards going across the magnificent mahogany desk of Lippincott's private secretary, driving her back into a Picasso original. The office was like an art gallery, except that few galleries could afford this collection of Picassos, Matisses, Renoirs and Chagalls. Remo grabbed a blue picture with many dots off the wall and led his group to see Mr. Lippincott himself. A guard protested, so Remo left him behind—with his head in a bookcase.

The office of Laurence Butler Lippincott had no door. None was needed, Remo realized. The door was really back down at the 60th floor.

Lippincott looked up from a typewritten page he was reading. He was a graying elderly man, with taut skin and the placid confidence of the very rich in his face.

"Yes?" he said, apparently undisturbed by the commotion.

"My name is Remo and I say no."

"Mr. Lippincott," the briefcase man tried to explain while clinging to a splintered arm, but he did not have a chance to finish because he was flying over his employer's head. Lippincott scarcely noticed.

"Really, Mr. Mueller, must you? The man is injured."

So Remo threw the sixieth-floor manager at Lippincott.

"If something is on your mind, say it," said Lippincott. "No need to hurt innocent people."

Remo placed one of the bodyguards on Lippincott's desk, which surprisingly looked very ordinary, right down to the pictures of family. Remo knocked the air out of the bodyguard. Lippincott merely removed the typewritten sheet from beneath him.

Remo placed the second bodyguard, who had suddenly tried to break for the door, on top of the first. He too suddenly lost his breath.

"You're trying to tell me something," Lippincott suggested.

"Yes," said Remo.

"You're trying to tell me that all my employees and all my money won't do me any good with you."

"Yes," said Remo.

"Are you also threatening me with physical violence if I should attempt to send others?"

"Yes," said Remo.

"Sounds reasonable," said Lippincott. "Would you care for something to drink?"

"No thanks," said Remo.

"Cigar?"

"No thanks," said Remo.

"A fifteenth of Venezuela?"

"No thanks," said Remo.

"Is there anything I can give you?"

"Leave me alone."

"You're sure we can't make some sort of deal?"

"Right."

"That sounds impossible," Lippincott said. "Everyone wants something. What do you want?"

"None of your business."

"Sounds reasonable although I don't understand it. If you should ever want anything of me, please let me know because I want your help and somehow I think I'll figure out a way to get it."

Remo heard a scream from outside and he saw Lippincott switch on an intercom.

"It's all right, Miss Watkins. No cause for alarm."

"There's a madman in your office, Mr. Lippincott."

"It's all right. First clear-talking man I've met since grandfather died."

"I'll get the police."

"Nonsense. Get a doctor. We have wounded men in here. We don't need the police." He switched off the intercom. "A pleasure meeting you, Mr. Mueller."

"Same here," said Remo.

"If only these clowns knew how to talk to people. That's the trouble with having so much money. Everybody thinks they know what you want and they don't bother to find out what you really want. They do all sorts of horrid things in your name. I take it you're all right."

"I'm fine," said Remo.

"You weren't going to destroy that Seurat, were you?"

"I was," said Remo, returning the painting with dots.

"To prove that money meant nothing to you, I suppose."

"Yes," said Remo.

"I'll buy it back."

"No need," said Remo. "It wasn't mine to begin with," and he left Lippincott's office feeling that if only people made their positions clear, half the problems in the world could be solved by reasonable men, reasoning together.

CHAPTER FOUR

When Remo returned to the Berkshires, upstairs had left a message. Chiun, who did not follow telephone codes, recognized the words "Aunt Mildred."

"Aunt Mildred what, Chiun?" asked Remo.

"Aunt Mildred. I do not play your little word games. If Dr. Smith wishes to see you, why doesn't he just say, 'I wish to see you?' Instead, Aunt Mildred is very sorry she cannot come or Aunt Mildred will have dinner ready or Aunt Mildred will refurnish the blue room."

"Do you remember which one?"

"I do not," said Chiun imperiously, as if Remo had overstepped his bounds by asking.

"I only ask because one of the things you mentioned means we should run for our lives and another means that everything is hunky dory."

"Running for one's life is the surest way to lose it."

"That's not the point, Chiun. It's that they mean different things."

"They mean nothing to me."

"But they mean something to me."

"Then you should be here to answer the telephone instead of fulfilling boasts," answered Chiun, thus closing the conversation to his satisfaction.

Remo waited until early dawn for the phone to ring again, but it did not, and he was about to nap when he heard a car pull up to the driveway. Just by the slow, careful and neat way it parked, by the careful opening of the door so as not to wear the hinges unduly, Remo knew that it was upstairs, Dr. Harold W. Smith, director of CURE. The message must have been Aunt Mildred will have dinner ready. That meant stay where you are. Will contact in person.

"I see Chiun got the message correct," said Smith, not bothering to thank Remo for opening the door or even acknowledging his greeting. "You really shouldn't complain that he can't relay codes. He did very well this time. You're here."

Smith wore a dark suit and a white shirt and striped tie. With the crispness of a mail clerk he walked onto the sun porch. The sun was sending little red cracks into the gray early morning sky over Lake Patusick.

"I don't suppose you have any coffee," asked Smith.

"Right. We don't have coffee. Want some cold duck?"

"Alcohol this early?"

"No alcohol. Leftover duck from last night's dinner."

"Sounds awful," Smith said.

"Tastes worse."

Remo eyed Smith and the small bulge in his left jacket pocket that looked like an overstuffed envelope. He wondered how many people played small unknowing roles in collecting what went into that envelope . . . a secretary who made an extra income by adding a file in a magazine office that said Remo Mueller was a writer who could be counted on for Africa stories . . . a banker who a month before had quietly opened a bank account and a line of credit for a man he had never seen, but whose name was Remo Mueller and who came highly recommended by friends. CURE was in that envelope, hundreds of people doing little jobs and not knowing the overall picture.

"I see you're interested in the envelope. Your tickets to Busati and your passports are in here along with an article under your byline. You should read it. You wrote it."

"I read it," said Remo.

"It hasn't been published yet."

"Some clown who works for Lippincott showed it to me. They offered to hire me."

"Excellent. Beyond my fondest hopes. Perfect. We had planned to get you into Busati as a journalist, let the blame fall on the magazine. But working for Lippincott is even better. For the first time, Remo, I see operations proceeding even better than planned, which is unusual for you."

"I won't be working for Lippincott," Remo said. "I sort of explained to him that I couldn't."

"You met Laurence Butler Lippincott?" asked Smith, with a tinge of reverence in his voice that Remo resented.

"Yeah. I met Lippincott. I threw a few of his employees at him."

"You what?"

"I told him I didn't want to work for him."

"But he'd make an excellent cover. We need someone to take the heat if you get messy in Busati."

Remo shrugged.

"You haven't even been committed yet," Smith groused, "and you've already created your first foul-up."

"So, don't commit me," said Remo and left the sunporch for the refrigerator where he grabbed the carcass of a cold duck and a bowl of cold rice and, against previous warnings by Chiun, ate even though his mind was not at peace. Smith had followed him into the kitchen.

Remo tore off a greasy drumstick and began to chew the mouthful into liquid. The problem, Smith explained, was not just that James Forsythe Lippincott was missing in the Africa bush. Those things happened. CURE wouldn't bother to get involved for that, not even for a Lippincott. No, a dangerous pattern was emerging. Very dangerous.

Remo took a little ball of rice between his fingertips and placed it into his mouth. How he would love a hamburger, he thought.

"A pattern that could undermine the American people's faith in the ability of its government to protect them," Smith said.

Perhaps if he mixed the rice and duck together in his mouth, thought Remo, it might taste better.

"The basis of any government is the protection it gives its citizens," Smith said.

Remo tried mixing a sliver of duck with a few grains of rice.

"We don't have final proof, but we believe that someone is raiding America for slaves."

Perhaps if Remo washed down the duck and the rice with warm water. Maybe that would improve it.

"In the last year, several wealthy young girls from branches of the Lippincott family have met violent deaths. Or at least we thought they had. But now we have found out that the girls did not really die. In their coffins there were other bodies. We believe someone is somehow smuggling these girls out of the country to Africa, as slaves. Sort of a reverse slavery."

Remo turned the water faucet on hot and filled a glass. He sipped it and that didn't help either.

"Reverse slavery?" he asked.

"Yes," Smith said. "Blacks taking whites."

"Doesn't sound reverse to me," said Remo. "It's slavery."

"Correct," Smith said. "It's just that historically, whites took blacks."

"Only an idiot lives in history," said Remo repeating something Chiun had once told him and which he had never understood.

"Right," Smith said. "It's really a rather simple sort of operation. Get into Busati, find out what happened to the missing Lippincott, free the girls, and get out."

"Why not do it through the government?"

"We can't," Smith said. "Our sources indicate that General Obode, the President of Busati, is somehow behind this. If we try to approach him directly, he'll just kill the girls. No. We've got to get them freed first. Then our government can deal with Obode, and he can't lie his way out."

"Can I kill Obode?"

Smith shook his head. "Too risky. He's a nut, but he's our nut. Killing him might cause us real problems in that part of the world."

"You say your sources say that Obode's in it. How good are your sources?" Remo said.

"Impeccable," Smith said. "CIA type sources."

"Do your sources know where the girls are?"

"No. All we've heard is that there's a white house with an iron gate in the capital city of Busati."

"You don't know though, right?"

"Correct."

"And you don't know how the girls are being kidnaped, right?"

"Correct."

"And you were trying to get me fixed up with Lippincott, but you didn't tell me you were doing it, right?"

"Right," said Smith.

Remo returned the duck and the rice to the refrigerator. Nothing would improve its taste.

"You know, Smitty," he said, "nothing works right in America anymore. Nothing."

CHAPTER FIVE

President General Dada "Big Daddy" Obode would see no one that morning. The stars were wrong. Hadn't a jackal made its way into the palace grounds the night before and howled three times, yet no one saw the jackal? Where was the jackal? This he demanded out loud on the balcony of his sitting room, once the sitting room of the former British governor—whom Big Daddy had served as a sergeant major in Her Majesty's Kenya Rifles.

"Where is the jackal?" he yelled. And had not the elephants at the Busati Army compound been seen wandering, even before the dry season? Why were they wandering? Who were they looking for? And what of the Minister of Public Safety who had been found nailed to a tree?

General Obode asked these questions of himself and there was no answer. His wise men were not wise, his generals were not courageous, his counselors lacked counsel.

He walked before a large ornate mirror, and looked at his massive frame and his thick dark features. A Hausa among Hausa he was.

"Dada, I ask you to search your heart with honesty

and truth," he said to his image in the mirror. "Is it possible that you are the cause of your own problems? Be honest now, because I will brook no deceit, especially from you, you . . . sergeant major."

General Obode furrowed his brows and thought. He thought a very long time. He looked at his gold watch. Fifteen seconds. Enough thought. He had the answer.

"It is not your fault, General Obode. You are a good leader. It is the fault of your enemies. Destroy your enemies and you will destroy he who was responsible for the jackal."

With that he clapped his hands for his clothes, changed his mind and decided he would hold his morning audience. There was a full schedule today. The Ambassador from Libya—that was important because of the money; the representative of the Third World Liberation Organization—that was unimportant because all they did was talk and there were a lot of yellow men. He did not trust yellow men any more than he trusted Indians or white men, at least those white men who were not English officers.

He liked English officers. English officers never bothered anyone, especially during operations when they knew they would muck things up and so left the business in the hands of sergeants major who knew how to get things done. He thought another ten seconds and decided he did not like Arabs either, even though he had been a Moslem from birth.

"Who do you like—honestly, General Obode?" he asked himself.

"I like you, big fella," he said. "You're all right." With that he laughed a booming laugh and laughed, while servants put on his boots and white uniform pants and shirts with the medals and general's pips on the shoulders.

When he was ready for the day, he called for Colonel William Forsythe Butler, who had been insisting that the general see a magazine writer named Remo Mueller, because Remo Mueller had written a nice story about General Obode and nice stories were rare nowadays.

"Nice story today, bad story tomorrow, to hell with him," General Obode had told his American-born chief of staff, who had all sorts of mixed blood mucking up his veins and who called himself black. He was a clever one though, this Colonel William Forsythe Butler. A good man to have around. He was not a Hausa, so he would not be jealous of General Obode's magnificence; he was not a Loni, so he would not hate General Obode for no reason at all. He was, he once had explained, "just an American nigger, but I'm working on that."

A good man. General Obode would humor him. Today, he would try to see this pipsqueak writer with the funny name of Remo.

Colonel William Forsythe Butler was the first to enter. He appeared thin, but General Obode knew him to be a most powerful man, the only one in Busati to have wrestled him to a draw one afternoon, after Obode threw two generals and three sergeants simultaneously before the cheers of his troops. He had been a football player, this Colonel Butler, Morgan State, and then the New York Mammoths—or was it the New York Giants? These names Americans had were all peculiar.

"Good morning, Colonel," said General Obode, sitting down in the ornate high-backed governor's chair which was now the president's chair. "Did you hear the jackal last night?"

"I did, Mr. President."

"And what would you make of a jackal in America if it howled at night? Three times?"

"We don't have jackals in America."

"Aha," said General Obode, clapping his hands. "And we do not have jackals in the palace grounds, either. Then what would you make of a jackal in your New York City?"

"I would think it strange, Mr. President."

"And so do I. I will teach you another lesson in governing that even your CIA didn't teach you."

"It would be an honor to learn, Mr. President."

General Obode clapped his hands and in marched eight men in neat Western suits and neat Western shirts and neat Western ties. When they talked, they talked in neat British accents. They were Obode's civilian council of state to whom he gave no power at all, preferring to surround himself in important jobs with military men. Six of the civilian council were Hausa, the other two were Loni, appointed reluctantly by Obode at Butler's urging. Butler had told him that the Western world would recognize this as an act of greatness, assimilating into his government the members of a once hated and hunted enemy tribe.

"A jackal howled three times last night," announced Obode. "Now to you Oxford and Cambridge people, it is nothing. And I'm sure it is nothing at some fancy United Nations office where all they have to do is worry about the air conditioning staying on. But this American here, this Butler, who has come home to his rightful land, he thinks it is something and he is CIA formerly. Now all of you have heard of the Central Intelligence

Agency. It is not Oxford. It is not Cambridge. It is not the United Nations."

"It is a vicious, dangerous organization, Mr. President," said the chairman of the council who was a Hausa. "It will stop at nothing to achieve its ends."

"Right," said General Obode. "Therefore we can have some respect for it. And this former CIA man tells me a jackal howling at night is something strange. What do you think?"

While Obode spoke, Butler looked down at the floor, his left fingers twisting a ring he wore on his right hand, a ring fashioned of miniature golden chain links.

It was the consensus of the council that the howling jackal was definitely strange. The strangest thing they had ever heard of.

"Not the strangest thing," said General Obode angrily. "A strange thing. We will investigate CIA style."

He dismissed the council with a wave of his hand. Seven of them, while leaving, caught Colonel Butler's eye with a conspiratorial look, the look one gives a partner one trusts when there is really nothing to talk about.

Obode summoned the captain of the palace guard who was a Hausa, and whose hatred of Butler fairly oozed as he entered the president's quarters and saw the American there. The captain had also heard the jackal last night, and he had arrested a lieutenant for imitating the animal, just to intimidate the president.

"From the Loni," said the captain, looking at Butler. "This lieutenant was a Loni and he was the jackal."

"Let us see this jackal," said General Obode. When the captain of the guard left, Obode explained his logic to Butler. Jackals did not live in the palace. Soldiers did. Therefore the jackal was a soldier.

"I don't think so," said Colonel Butler.

"What is your rank, Butler?"

"Colonel, Mr. President."

"And what is my rank?"

"General, Mr. President."

"Did they teach you discipline in your CIA?"

"They did."

"Then you know that when a colonel disagrees with a general, a general is right." Big Daddy clapped his hands gleefully.

"No, Mr. President, they taught me that the general gets his way. But any man can be right."

Obode frowned, a deep dark frown. He summoned Butler's ear forward with a finger.

"When I want logic, Butler, I'll ask for it," he said.

"The lieutenant is innocent, though," whispered Butler, hearing the captain again approach the door.

"Maybe he is, maybe he isn't. He could be the jackal."

"He's not," Butler said. "I am the jackal."

Obode leaned back and stared at Butler. "You want to die, Colonel?"

"No, Mr. President, I want your life saved. I brought the jackal into the palace last night to root out your enemies. If I put the jackal there, whoever says he found a man to be the jackal is a liar. The captain of your guard is a liar. He knows that you want to bring the Loni into the government, and so he is trying to destroy your plan by accusing the Loni lieutenant of a crime he did not commit. You see your enemy? He is as far away as the captain."

Obode did not look up at the captain who was now approaching the President's chair. Intrigue was afoot.

Butler looked at the captain, who returned his look with loathing. Butler winked. The captain had been one of the few men close to Obode who did not agree with Butler that Obode was a lunatic whose continued rule would make Busati a worldwide joke. Because the captain did not agree with Butler, the captain was dangerous to Butler. But now he had overplayed his hand.

The captain stood in front of Obode with a hand on the shoulder of a thin man, wearing the tattered remnants of a lieutenant's uniform. The man's legs and wrists were in heavy gray irons. His mouth was a blotch of blood. A tooth stuck out through his lower lip.

"He has confessed that he is the jackal, General," said the captain.

"A confession is a confession," said Obode. "That is logic and the CIA style of investigation is logic, so the man is guilty. But I will ask him myself."

Obode looked up at the lieutenant, who had to be continually jerked upright by the captain of the guards.

"Are you the jackal?"

Drops of dark red blood fell to the clean marble floor at the man's feet, building a puddle, splattering faint rays of red around it as each drop hit. The man, his eyes swollen almost shut, nodded and the puddle became bigger.

Butler twisted the gold chain ring on his right hand.

"Guilty," said Obode. The captain smiled.

"Set up a firing squad," said Obode. "I will personally administer the execution." He clapped his hands, the man was led away, and servants rushed in with rags and water to clean the blood off the palace floor.

Big Daddy took care of the Libyan Ambassador in three minutes. He confided to the Ambassador that Israel was planning a raid on the Busati plain and he needed $85 million more in gold reserves to repel it. When the Libyan ambassador appeared somewhat dubious, Big Daddy wistfully remembered the fine training he had personally received from the Israeli paratroopers and how he longed to wear again the wings he had earned at such a high personal cost. He also reminded the Ambassador that he was the only leader of a nation to publicly say to the foreign press that Hitler had been right. That was worth at least $85 million right there. The Libyan Ambassador timidly suggested that Big Daddy had been paid for that already, but finally agreed to ask his glorious revolutionary leader, Colonel Quadaffi, for the funds.

"Don't ask—tell," said Obode and that took care of the Libyan Ambassador.

"We'll get $25 million," Obode told Butler when the Ambassador had left. "Better than nothing. I can't wait for their oil to dry up. They smell funny. Who's next?"

"The journalist, Remo Mueller, from America. The one who wrote the favorable piece about you," said Butler.

"I'll see him tomorrow."

"You've been saying that for three days."

"I'll say that for three days more. We have an execution for me to administer. But first I wish to see the jackal you say you brought into the grounds."

"Will you still execute the lieutenant?"

"I said there would be an execution. I cannot go back on my word," said Obode.

The salutes along the corridors by the guards were crisp and rigid, a perfection of discipline that could only be imposed by the best of British sergeants major.

As they walked down steps to a small cell beneath the

palace, Obode asked Butler how things were at the white house with the iron gate.

"Just fine, Mr. President. Your soldiers who use it bless your name continuously. You should pay it a visit yourself."

Obode sneered and shook his head.

"You don't like white women, General?"

"You don't have to put them in chains to bang them. I will tell you, Colonel, that before you came I had white women. I had yellow women. I had Hausa women and Loni women. I had old women and young women, fat women and skinny women, women who smelled of perfume and women who smelled of dung. Colonel Butler," said Obode, pausing before an iron door to which Butler had the key, "there isn't a spit's difference between any of them. And your adventures to get young rich American girls costs too much, and may yet get us into trouble with your American government."

"But, General, isn't it fitting that the greatest soldiers of the great leader of a great country, get the very best?"

"Best of what? Queen Elizabeth or the lowest bush tribe whore. Same thing."

"You have had Queen Elizabeth?"

"No. But if a man eats one hundred hogs, does he have to eat another to know what it will taste like?"

"I'm sorry, General, I thought you approved of what I was doing for your men." Butler twisted the gold ring on his right hand.

Obode shrugged his massive shoulders. "You wanted to have your house and your games so I let you. I like you, Butler. You are the only man on my staff who has not loyalty to one tribe or another, but is loyal just to me. Even if you *are* soft on the Loni. So, I let you have your house. Now let me see your jackal."

Butler turned the key and opened the door on an empty cell. Obode walked in and sniffed the air. Before the stunned Butler could move, Obode snapped the Colonel's revolver from his holster as if disarming a recalcitrant enlisted man.

"I put the jackal here myself. I tied it right to that wall. I wanted to show you there were liars in your guard. The jackal was here, General. What reason would I have to lie to you?"

"Outside, Butler," said Obode.

The palace courtyard was hot in the morning African sun, baking hot with dust in the very grass itself. The captain of the guard grinned broadly when he saw the Loni-loving American Colonel go before the General with his hands up and holster empty. He winked broadly at Butler, and then turned and motioned his firing squad to kneel.

"Against the wall," said General Obode.

At the wall, Butler spun around beside the Loni officer who was chained against the wall in a standing position, but whose body hung heavy from his wrist manacles.

"You're a damned idiot, General," Butler yelled. "When you shoot me, you shoot the best officer you have. I just want you to know that, you dumb bastard."

"You call me a dumb bastard," yelled back Obode, "but you're the one who's got his hands up against the wall."

At that, Butler laughed.

"You're right, you fat bastard, but you're still shooting the best officer you ever had."

"That's where you're wrong, skinny little man. I am going to shoot the officer who lied to me about the jackal."

The captain of the guard smiled. The firing squad behind him waited for a signal. It did not get one. There was the crack of a pistol and the captain of the palace guard was no longer smiling. There was a very dumb look on his face and a very wide dark red hole between his eyes, although few people saw it because the head was jerked back by the force of the shot. The body followed. It hit the burned grass with a whoomph and moved no more.

"So much for people who lie to me about jackals. And now for those who call me a fat bastard," said General Obode. He extended the pistol at arm's length and walked up to Colonel Butler's face.

"Don't do it again," he said to Butler and spun the pistol around, Western style, offering it handle first.

"How do you know I won't shoot you now, you? . . ." said Butler, stopping as the pistol spun once more in Obode's hand so that now Butler was again looking down the barrel.

". . . glorious leader," smiled Butler, finishing the sentence.

"You and you," Obode yelled to two soldiers still kneeling, waiting for an execution order. "Take that man down from the wall. And treat him carefully. He is your new captain of the palace guard."

"He is a Loni," Butler said, taking the pistol from Obode and returning it to his holster.

"The other one was a Hausa, and he lied to me. How much worse could a Loni be?"

As he and Butler walked from the courtyard, Obode

said, "You looked funny when that cell was empty. Did you look funny! Did you really think, though, that anyone could hide a jackal smell from me? Especially when the Hausa custom is that the chief must protect himself when the jackal howls at night?"

"I have a nose too, General. I smelled nothing but disinfectant in that call."

"Right," said Obode. "And who would wash a cell with disinfectant unless he was trying to hide a smell? The captain obviously found your jackal and disposed of it. I tell you, if more generals were sergeant majors, the world would be a better place." He paused and said, "I wonder if that captain was responsible for killing the Minister of Public Safety."

Butler shrugged. "Maybe," he said. "And maybe we'll never know. Anyway, now that we know the jackal wasn't magic, General, perhaps we can get on to other things."

Obode shook his head slowly, as he turned and led Butler down a graveled path leading into the heavily-treed palace grounds.

"You think because one thing I believe in is disproven, I should not believe in anything I know to be true? Wrong. Because one of America's missiles doesn't work, do they stop building missiles? No. Because they know the majority of missiles are good. These are strange times in Busati, Butler. We are not rich and advanced like in Kenya or Zaire. But there are things one does not learn in universities. These things I know."

"I do not understand," said Butler. He saw a lizard scurry under a bush. For that lizard to brave the noonday African sun meant there must be a predator about, probably a rodent of some sort. This Butler had learned from Obode.

"Why do you think I have expelled all the Asians?" Obode asked. "Why do you think I expelled all the whites? The whole world thinks, here goes Big Daddy being cruel to whites and Asians he needs for his economy. Oh, what a crazy man is this Dada Obode. That is what they think. I know that. I am not a fool. Why do you think I did those things?"

"I don't know, General."

Big Daddy paused by a large wide mango tree, like the one Colonel Butler had nailed the Minister of Public Safety to, like the one Butler had killed James Forsythe Lippincott under, like the ones which stood before the hills where the Loni hid. Butler looked absent-mindedly for the predator to follow the lizard into the bush. But he saw no predator.

"It is all connected, Butler. All of it. And there is a reason for all the things I do."

Butler nodded, still wondering where the predator was. He saw the lizard's tail sticking out from under the bush, motionless.

"You do not know the Loni," Obode said. "Today, they are just a weak collection of spineless mountain bands, but once they were powerful. Once they ruled the Hausa as we now rule them. But there is a legend that says the Loni will again come to power. The legend says that when East and West are like father and son near the Busati River, then a force that no man can stop will come to shed blood in the river and in the mountains."

Butler nodded.

"You nod, but I do not think you understand, Colonel. The legend says that the Loni children will come home. It says a man from the East will purify the Loni and make them again worthy to rule. And it says a man from the West, a man who walks in the shoes of death, will rid the Loni of a man who would enslave them."

"And you're the man who would enslave the Loni?" Butler asked.

Obode shrugged his shoulders. "Who else could the legend mean but the Hausa man who is the leader of the country? You wonder why I have listened to you and put Loni men into my government? I have done it because I want to be free of the title of 'man who would enslave them.' But still I fear. I do not think that one can outsmart a legend."

"I see." Butler watched the lizard's tail poke out of the bush. When General Obode went into one of his prophecy raves, the best thing to do was to nod.

"Perhaps you are beginning to see," Obode said.

"The legend says a man from the East and a man from the West. Yellow and white. To serve the Loni. And if that happens, the Hausa are through and I am dead. That is why I got rid of our Asians. That is why I got rid of our whites. I do not want yellow men and white men joining, lest they become this force to free the Loni. You see?"

Butler, who had his own very good ideas on what the legend meant and how it was soon to be fulfilled, simply nodded at Obode's explanation. Where was the predator? Why was that lizard's tail still sticking out of that bush?

"Butler," said Obode. "I think there are times when there are some things you not only fail to understand, but you refuse to try understanding."

"I'm only a colonel," Butler said.

"All right. Now you're a general. You must understand everything now. Understand this, General. I take no chances with the Loni legend. I do not want Westerners in Busati. I do not want this Remo Mueller. I do not want any more of your white women from America."

"As one general to another, Big Daddy, let me say I've got to have one more."

"Get one from China."

"No. It's got to be America. It's got to be a certain one."

"No more," said Obode.

"This one is the most important one. I've got to get her. If you say no, I'll resign."

"Over a white woman?"

"A special one."

Obode thought deeply for a few seconds. He cupped his chin in his ham-wide, cave-black hands. "All right. But this is the last."

"After her, General, I will want no more. She makes it all perfect."

"And you say I am hard to understand," said Obode. "One last thing, General Butler. Do not think the legends are all lies or that General Obode is a fool."

He put a heavy hand on Butler's shoulder. "Come, I will show you something you do not think I know. You have been watching that tail under the bush, you think there is no predator around because you do not see one. You think the lizard ran into the sun for no reason, right?"

"Well, yes, I guess that's what I was thinking," said Butler, surprised that Obode had seen his interest in the bush.

"Good. Good to show you a point. Even if you cannot see something, it does not mean that it does not exist. There is a predator around."

"I saw no rats or birds. I still see the tail."

Obode smiled. "Yes, you see the tail. But come quickly or you will not see it."

When they reached the bush, Obode drew aside the green foliage. "Look," he said, smiling.

Butler looked. He had seen a tail all right, but that was all that was left of the lizard, sticking from the full mouth of a very fat frog.

"Sometimes when you run from danger, you run to it," said Obode, but he forgot the lesson very quickly that afternoon when he again not only refused to see the writer, Remo Mueller, but ordered him evicted from Busati. Immediately.

CHAPTER SIX

The Busati Hotel had air conditioning that did not work, faucets that gave no water, and elegant carpeting with inlaid old food. The rooms were like furnaces, the hallways smelled like sewers and the only remnant of its former grandeur was a clean brochure with Victoria Hotel scratched out and Busati Hotel penciled in.

"Spacious, air conditioned and elegant, the Busati Hotel offers the finest conveniences and the most gracious service in all East Africa," read Remo.

Chiun sat on the floor, his white robe flowing and motionless behind him. Remo sat on the edge of the bed with the high brass posters.

"I've heard of untruth in advertising," said Remo, "but this is a bit much."

Chiun did not answer.

"I said this is a bit much."

Chiun remained a silent statue.

"Little Father, there is no television set before you. You're not watching your shows. So why don't you answer me?"

"But I am watching my shows," said Chiun. "I am remembering them."

Remo was surprised that he shared a bit of Chiun's

anguish at the master's loss of the daytime soap operas. They had been a constant nettle to Remo through the years, but now that they were gone, he felt sorry for the Master of Sinanju.

"That Watergate thing will not last, Chiun. All your shows will return."

"I know that," said Chiun.

"So you don't really have to sit staring at a wall."

"I am not staring at a wall. I am remembering. He who can remember the good things as though they were present can live his happiness forever."

"Well, let me know when you stop remembering, so we can talk."

Remo looked at his wristwatch. At home, Chiun's soap operas went off at 3:30. He would time Chiun and see how close he came to judging the time.

At 3:27 by Remo's watch, Chiun toward turned him.

"You missed, Chiun."

"Missed? What stupidity are you pursuing now?"

"The shows go off at 3:30. And it's only 3:27 and you were done," Remo said triumphantly. "Three minutes off. A child could have a better sense of time than that. Three minutes is a long time."

"Three minutes is not very long in the life of one who has dedicated every minute to foolishness," Chiun said.

"Meaning?"

"Meaning, you forgot the moments of selling. I do not watch them. I do not use soap powder."

Chagrined because he had indeed forgotten the three minutes of commercials at the end of the day's stories, Remo said, "Yeah, well, anyway, I was talking about the brochure."

"It may not be a lie," Chiun said.

"Look around you, it's not a lie?"

"I look around and I see that perhaps at one time it was the truth. I see elegance in decay. So if these things were said about this palace when they were true, then the advertisement is true."

"Are you telling me, Little Father, that to say this is a stinkhole is a lie?"

"I am telling you that truth is a matter of time. Even in this very land there are people who were once great and who now hide in the hills like frightened calves."

"Well, I don't need that drivel now, Chiun. I need advice. I'm supposed to see the top man in this country to find out about that white house, without letting him know that I know. But he won't see me."

Chiun nodded. "Then my advice to you is to forget all your training and run head first like a crazed dog into what you, in your lack of perception, think is the center of things. There, thrash about like a drunken white man, and then, at the moment of maximum danger, remember just a brief part of the magnificent training of Sinanju, and save your worthless life. At the end of this disgrace, you might by good fortune have killed the right man. This then is the advice of the Master of Sinanju."

Remo blinked. He stood up from the bed.

"That's utterly stupid, Chiun."

"I just wanted for once to give you advice I am sure you would follow. But since I have invested such wealth of knowledge with you, I shall increase this investment. You think because the emperor appears to be the center of things, he is the center of things."

"It's president, not emperor."

"Whatever name you wish to give to an emperor is your pleasure, my son, but emperors do not change in nature. And what I am saying to you is that you must know the center of this thing before you can attack it. You are not an army that goes blindly wandering through bush and hill and can by sheer weight of numbers accidentally accomplish what it wants. You are skill, a single skill that is designed to crush one point, not ten thousand. Therefore you must know that point."

"How can I find that point waiting around here in this crummy hotel?"

"A man sitting sees many sides very well. A man running sees only ahead."

"I see many sides when I run. You taught me that."

"When you run with your feet," said Chiun, and was silent. Remo left the room to see if he could find something to read, someone to talk to, or even a vagrant breeze to get into the middle of. He was unsuccessful. But at the stately doors of the hotel, he saw a busboy run desperately past him with fear in his eyes. The manager of the hotel hid the books. The doorman snapped to attention.

And then Remo saw it. Coming up the main street of the capital city of Busati, an army convoy, machine guns bristling from jeeps. Leading it was the man who had extended the invitation that writer Remo Mueller see General Obode.

When the lead jeep of the convoy arrived at the doors of the Hotel Busati, it stopped in a screech of dust off the unpaved street. Soldiers jumped off their jeeps all along the line before their vehicles braked.

"Ah, Remo, glad to see you," said now-General William Forsythe Butler, quickly climbing the once-white front steps of the hotel. "I've got a bit of bad news for you. The bit is you're returning to America this afternoon. But I've got some good news for you too."

Remo smiled perfunctorily.

"The good news is I'll be going with you and I'd be happy to answer every question you have. As a matter of fact, Busati feels it owes you a favor which it hopes to repay."

"By kicking me out of the country?"

"President Obode has had some very disappointing experiences with white journalists."

"Then why'd you say I could get to see him?"

"I thought I could prevail upon him but I couldn't." Butler shrugged, a big muscular shrug of his shoulders. "We'll talk about it some more on the way to the airport."

Frankly, Butler was relieved that this Remo Mueller would be leaving the country since the fewer Americans there were nosing around, the less chance of the white house being discovered. That relief only grew when he got his first look at Remo Mueller's traveling companion, an aged Oriental who padded silently out of the Busati Hotel behind Remo, acknowledged Butler's lukewarm greeting with a silent stare, and sat like stone in the back seat of the jeep.

What was it Obode had said? "When East and West are like father and son near the Busati River, then a force that no man can stop will come to shed blood in the river and on the mountains."

East and West. The aged Oriental and the young white American.

Butler could do without Remo and the Oriental. He had his own interpretations of the legend . . . an interpretation that he knew would carry him to the Busatian presidential palace, and power over all the people of all the tribes.

He thought about this in silence as the jeep convoy rolled toward the airport, and then realized he was being a bad host.

It was where the road banked in along the Busati River, that he turned toward the back seat to see how his passengers were doing.

They were gone.

"What the hell?" said Butler. "Stop the damned convoy."

He looked at his driver, then looked back to the rear seats. They were indeed empty.

"Did you see them jump out?" asked Butler, almost as a reprimand.

"No, General," said the driver. "I didn't know they were gone. We were doing forty-five miles an hour, General."

The long convoy bunched up into tightly packed jeeps as it stopped on Busati's Route One and Only, which ran from the capital city to the airport. Butler could see for a half-mile in each direction. There was no sign of them.

"Their bodies must be up the road no more than a hundred meters or so, General."

Butler stood up in the jeep signaling to the vehicle cramped in tight behind him.

"Sergeant, did you see our passengers?"

"Sir?" called out the sergeant.

"The white man and the Oriental. Did you see them jump from the jeep?"

The sergeant threw the snappy kind of British salute

Butler hated so much. He used the word "sir" to punctuate his reply.

"Sir, no sir. No passengers observed leaving your vehicle, sir."

"Form search parties and scour the road. Fan out. Find them. They do not know this earth."

"Sir, very good, sir," said the sergeant.

But Remo and Chiun were not found, although it came to be believed that at least five men might have stumbled on them or on something, because the necks of the five were broken and they lay peacefully in search formation, the safeties off their rifles and their fingers on the feather-light triggers, as though a breeze of death had gently put them to sleep.

Three other men were missing, one of them a captain, but General Butler would not wait. He would not have waited if the gates of hell opened before him. He was going to catch a plane for America to settle the last payment on a three-hundred-year-old debt, and when that had been collected, the world might see greatness as it had not for thousands of years.

At the airport, Butler told his personal Army detachment to continue the search for the Oriental and the American and to hold them in custody until he got back. "I shall be back in two days," he said, and with that walked quickly to the loading ramp of the Air Busati 707, with British pilots and navigators.

Three years before, in an advertisement for Air Busati, two Hausas posed in pilots' uniforms for photographs and the planes emptied of passengers in less than a minute, most of the passengers being Hausas too.

This Butler remembered as he entered the plane on

which he would be the only passenger and headed for the lounge in the back to change from his military uniform. Butler remembered the advertisement well. It did not appear in any African newspaper for fear of losing Air Busati the few passengers it had, but it made quite a hit in *The New York Times* where one militant several days later had called on the Busati Air Force to launch an immediate strike against South Africa.

The militant had held up the advertisement as he said: "Why don't these black pilots spearhead an attack on racist South Africa? I will tell you why. Because capitalism forces them to fly commercial airliners."

Butler had almost cried when he saw the news story about the militant, and when he thought that black men did indeed fly fighter aircraft—in America.

As the 707 jet rose sharply into the darkening Busati sky for the first leg of its journey to Kennedy Airport in New York City Willian Forsythe Butler leaned back in a reclining seat, aware that he was making his last trip west to a land to which centuries before his ancestors had been transported, shackled in the holds of ships built for carrying cattle.

Those trips had taken months. Many had died and many had thrown themselves overboard when they had a chance. They had come from many tribes—Loni, Hausa, Ashanti, Dahomey—and they would surrender this heritage to become a new people called "nigger." Few would ever find their way home.

William Forsythe Butler had found his way home. In the depths of his bitterness, he had found his home and his tribe and his people, and a curious legend that told him what he must do. Although, in truth, he had always been the kind of boy—then man—who seemed to know what he would do and how he would do it.

When he was eleven years old in Paterson, New Jersey, he suddenly realized he was very fast afoot, as fast as the wind. He was reading when this realization overcame him. He told his sister.

"Get outa here, Billie, you're a fat chubkins," she had said.

"I know, sis, I know. But I'm fast. I mean, I got the speed in me."

"I can outrun you, fatty," said his sister.

"Today, yeah. But not next month. And the month after that you won't even see me."

"Ain't nobody gonna move that flab fast, fatty," said his older sister.

But Billie Butler knew. All he would have to do would be to find that speed in himself. And he did. In football, he became high school All-American, and did the same at Morgan State.

His performance there was good enough to get him an offer from the Philadelphia Browns which, at the time, had an interesting way of judging football talent. They could have done it with a light meter. If you were black and fast and didn't come from a Big Ten school, you were a cornerback. And if your name was William Forsythe Butler, you became Willie Butler. Not Bill, not Billie, but Willie.

"I don't want to play defense," Butler had told them. "I want to play offense. I know I can play offense." But the Browns already had one black halfback. Butler became a cornerback.

He swallowed his pride and tried to look straight

ahead. He read about the black reawakening, which seemed to center around kids calling press conferences to announce imminent rebellions, which featured every sort of cuckoo in the black community being exalted by the white press as a black leader; and featured very few of his own people, the people who had sweat blood and tears and pain to wrest even the ownership of a home from a hostile land.

Just as he had known as a child that he had speed within him, he knew now what would happen in this still-hostile land of America.

He tried to explain to one militant he met on a plane.

"Look, if you're going to have a damned revolution, it might help not to announce your plans in *The New York Times*," he had said.

"Revolution is communication with the masses," the militant had said. "They must first be conscious that power comes from the barrel of a gun."

"Did it ever occur to you that the whites have most of the guns?"

"Whitey soft. He through. He dead, man."

"God help you if you ever back him into a corner," Butler told the youth, who responded that Butler was an Uncle Tom of a dead generation. Butler saw the name of the militant again one month later when the newspapers reported the youth had been arrested for holding up a drugstore.

Some of Butler's friends said this was a sign that the youth was really arrested for his political beliefs.

"Bullshit," said Butler. "If you know anything about how anything operates, that kid is just what you want for an enemy. He wasn't doing any harm to the government. He was really helping it."

"He was raising the consciousness of his people," said Butler's sister.

"Every time that kid opened his mouth, ten thousand whites moved to the right."

"That's a twisted way of thinking," said his sister. I don't know about you, but I'm tired of tomming."

"And I'm tired of losing. We're cutting off all our support in the north, and in the south, forget it."

"We got the Third World. We outnumber Whitey."

"Numbers don't count any more," Butler had said. "An army is made up of people who can work together and, most important, be in the right place at the right time. If I were running a black revolution in this country, I'd give the kids watches, not rifles."

"They really got to your head, didn't they, Mister not-allowed-to-carry-the-ball cornerback. And don't give me Whitey's talk about being wiped out. We been wiped out every century. And here we are."

"No," said Butler sadly, "I don't think we're going to be wiped out, because I don't think we can get up a good enough revolution right now to get wiped out. We're gonna be smothered in our own stupidity."

His sister's response was that Butler was too impressed with Whitey. Butler's answer was that Whitey wasn't all that good and pretty stupid himself, but that his sister made even the worst white cracker look like an intellectual giant.

Butler's despair deepened with almost every daily newspaper story about non-negotiable demands, the unity of the Third World and the talk of bullets. When departments of African studies were introduced across the land, William Forsythe Butler was at the point of tears. "The engineering schools, you dumb bastards," he would yell in the privacy of his apartment. "The engineering schools. That's survival."

Few of his friends spoke to him anymore, naturally, since he was an Uncle Tom without courage. Butler took it out on the gridiron. He was a cornerback with a vengeance, and he had a plan. One day, it all worked and Butler had a new team, the New York Giants, and a promise that he would be given a real shot at running back.

Opening day, he started the season at cornerback. He ended the season there.

It was then that William Forsythe Butler began to wonder if just maybe his sister weren't right.

The black consciousness movement was taking hold now in football and Butler became its spokesman. He did a statistical survey of the league that showed that more blacks than whites were jolted out of positions and put onto defensive teams.

He demanded to know why blacks got paid less for playing the same position as whites. Twentieth century slavery, he called it. He said that racism was the reason there wasn't a black quarterback, and announced that he would try out for that position the next year with his team.

These were the things Willie Butler talked about, but no answers came from organized football. Soon the sports pages froze him out of space, not wanting to do anything to damage the all-American spirit of the game.

And then one day, the back page of the *New York Daily News* bannered a headline that triggered in Butler a violent response and made him vow never to forget the slavery that had brought his forebears to the country. The headline read:

Butler first heard of it reading the paper, and rather than be sold anywhere by anyone, he retired from football.

He was still a young man, so he drifted into the Peace Corps, where he was shipped to Busati to try to develop an irrigation project that might raise a small parcel of the nation's land to its fertility level of two thousand years before. While working there, happy to be away from America, he was approached by the CIA man assigned to the Busati Peace Corps. The CIA man was going home; he had seen Butler at work and realized he was a true American; how would he like to work for the CIA?

For the extra money, Butler said *sure,* determined to screw up the intelligence apparatus by sending in ridiculous reports of non-occurring events and by predictions that bordered on the sublime.

In Busati's heat, the predictions all seemed to come true. Butler was put on full $36,000 salary by the CIA, assigned to help then-Colonel Obode, who was pro-West at the time, seize power.

About that time, William Forsythe Butler made a journey to the mountains of the Loni. As soon as he stepped into the first village, he knew he was home.

And he was ashamed of his home. The Loni were divided into small bands who hid in the hills; the men were timid little root-grubbers who spent their lives looking over their shoulders for the approach of the Hausa, or for oncoming elephants, or for anything larger than a lizard. The Loni Empire, probably because of the cowardice of its men, had turned into a matriarchy, the three major packs being led by three princess sisters. Butler met one sister and told her he knew he was a Loni.

How do we know you are not making up a story, he was asked.

And in his frustration, Butler made a hissing clicking sound in the back of his mouth as he had always done since childhood. The princess suddenly embraced Butler and welcomed him home.

Butler was confused.

The Princess explained that Loni men, when angered, always had made that hissing sound in their throats. She had not heard it in a long time.

Butler forgot about Obode and about his CIA assignment. He spent two weeks in the village where, for the first time, he heard the Loni legend. He had been brought up in a society which did not believe in legends, but even he thought there was enough in the legend that pertained to him.

The Loni children coming home. Well, wasn't he a Loni child who had come home?

And the man of the West, who was dead, killing the man who would enslave the Loni. Well, wasn't Butler from the West? And couldn't you call him dead, in a sense, because he had given up his former life to come live with the Loni? And the man who would enslave the Loni? Who else but Obode?

He did not understand anything about the Oriental who would redeem the Loni in the ritual flames, but who said legends had to be letter-perfect?

It was close enough to him to count And to show his brotherhood in blackness to the Loni people by repaying those who had taken them in slavery, and also to indulge himself a little bit, Butler decided to add something to the legend . . . the man who collected payment for a centuries-old sin.

He opened the briefcase on the seat next to him in the 707 jet and stared at the brown-cornered parchment, a ship's manifest, a load of slaves from East Africa. Another old parchment was a bill of sale. There was a yellowed fragment of paper from a plantation. Another fragment showed a family tree. And woven through all the documents were the names of the Lippincotts, the Butlers, the Forsythes: the three American families whose fortunes had been made in the slave trade.

From a small envelope he took a stack of newspaper clippings. The last one was a pretty little piece in the *Norfolk Pilot* about a Hillary Butler's engagement to a Harding Demster III. He hoped Harding Demster III would not be upset about waiting at the altar.

CHAPTER SEVEN

There had been trouble at the Busati Airport. According to the army detachment continuously assigned to Air Busati, largely to prevent the planes' tires and wheels from being stolen, seven large lacquered trunks were missing from the baggage terminal, and fourteen soldiers were unaccounted for.

The periodicals' stall had also been ransacked. It was believed that a riot had occurred in the stall because of the extensive damage, yet there were not enough people at the airport to cause such a riot. In fact, the only people there who were not Busatians were a white American and an aged Oriental, who had vanished along with the soldiers and the lacquered trunks.

"Do you think it is true?" asked General Obode of his personal valet, a fellow Hausa.

"About the riot?"

"About everything."

"You mean the East and the West, father and son?"

"Yes," said Obode.

The valet shook his head. "The Loni are in their mountains and there they shall stay. We should have no fear of a heartless mountain band. Especially now that you have begun to give them positions in the government. They shall not rise again. Fear not."

General Obode thought a minute. "Draw another $10,000 from the Ministry of the Treasury and deposit in my Swiss bank account," he said.

Meanwhile, across the Busati plains, a caravan plodded toward the mountains. Seven trunks on the shoulders of fourteen soldiers bobbed along the line, the sun glinting off their lacquered exteriors.

In front of this line marched the Master of Sinanju and Remo. Remo was furious.

"You're a damned two-faced sonuvabitch," he said.

"A contract is a contract," said Chiun. "A preceding unfilled contract always takes precedence over a more recent one. It is only fair."

"You're talking about a contract over two thousand years old. The House of Sinanju didn't even exist then, damned two-faced sonuvabitch."

"Name-calling no more obviates a contract than a few years here or there."

"This thing dates back before Christ. A few years. A few years, Little Father?"

"It is you who choose to date things from the time of Christ, not the House of Sinanju. We have an unfilled contract, paid for, mind you, paid in full. It was from the year of the ram. Or was it the year of the rat?"

"Probably from the year of the two-faced sonuvabitch."

"No matter. It was before the year of your 1950s or was it 1960s when the House of Sinanju agreed to train something dragged in off the streets, as a stopgap measure in lieu of a real assassin."

"May your autographed picture of Rad Rex be burned," said Remo.

Chiun looked back at the trunks and said something to one of the soldiers in what Chiun had explained was a Loni dialect. By the tone of the voice, Remo could tell Chiun was reminding the soldiers that the trunks contained valuables, probably that the first trunk contained the picture of Rad Rex, the star of *As the Planet Revolves,* and in case of emergency, it should be saved first.

It had shocked Remo when he had first heard Chiun speak this Loni tongue. He had thought the Master of Sinaju knew only Mandarin, Chinese, Japanese, Korean and some English.

But at the airport where he and Chiun had headed by foot after leaving General Butler in the jeep, Chiun had silenced him while moving to the airport gate. When they had gotten out of Butler's jeep, Remo had wanted to go right back to town to get on with the job of looking for the white house behind the iron gate. But Chiun had demanded they go to the airport and pick up Chiun's luggage. He would not negotiate or compromise. He wanted his luggage, he told Remo.

They did not know it but they reached the airport only minutes after Butler's airplane had taken off, and the permanent military detail at the airport was lounging around in the terminal when the two entered.

"I will speak to them in the language of the Loni Empire," Chiun said, "to find where our luggage is."

"The Loni? That's a tribe, Chiun."

"No, it is a great kingdom of great virtue," Chiun had said, which Remo took to mean that when they hired assassins they paid their bills on time.

"Well, let's get your luggage and get back to the capital. I've got work to do."

Chiun raised a long bony finger. The nail reflected the overhead light like a sliver of diamond. Chuin called to one of the guards in what sounded to Remo like the Swahili spoken as the main language of Busati.

"They're not going to talk to you, Chiun. We're foreigners."

"Speak for yourself, white man," had said the Master of Sinanju.

Remo crossed his arms and waited confidently for Chiun to get a rifle pointed at him by one of the guards. Let him fight his own way out, thought Remo. Perhaps there would even be a flaw in a stroke. That would be good to watch, even though Remo wasn't going to hold his breath waiting to see it.

Chiun spoke first in Loni dialect, then translated for Remo.

"I am the Master of Sinanju and this is Remo who is white but close to me. I tell them close, Remo, because they would not understand your natural disrespect and lack of appreciation. I would see your king for a debt I owe as a Master of Sinanju. Remo, they will know this, for it must be spoken of widely in their villages and temples that there is a debt owed by the Master of Sinanju."

The two guards conversed heatedly between themselves. Remo smiled.

"You mean to tell me, Little Father, that two African soldiers are going to remember a centuries-old contract by a foreign hitman."

"Try as you might, Remo, you will not understand the nature of Sinanju. The Loni know how to appreciate the services of the Masters of Sinanju, not like the Chinese emperors or the vile Americans."

Remo shook his head. When Chiun began on the glories of Sinanju, there was no reasoning with him. Perhaps five people in all the world had heard of the House of Sinanju—four of them must be in intelligence agencies and the fifth an obscure dust-covered historian. But to hear Chuin tell it, Sinanju was more important than the Roman Empire.

Chiun babbled on and the soldiers looked confused. They motioned for Remo and Chiun to follow them.

"You will see how a true people of dignity treat a Master of Sinanju," Chiun whispered proudly to Remo. "There are those with enough culture in the world to see a true assassin as more than a hitman as you call him. You will see."

"Chiun, you don't even know if these soldiers are Loni. They're probably going to shake us down."

"You have them confused with Americans," Chiun said.

The soldiers led Chiun and Remo to an officer where Chiun again explained something, hands moving unusually rapidly for just the telling of a story. Remo tried to discern from the officer's face what the reaction was, but the officer's night face was as changeless as space.

The officer pointed to a newstand inside the airport. Chiun nodded and beckoned to Remo.

"You'll see. You'll see what true respect is," he said. "Follow me."

Remo shrugged. The air terminal—slightly smaller than the one in Dayton, Ohio—was five times too big for the passenger use. Remo waited with Chiun at a periodical stand which had mostly English language publications.

"We'll store your luggage, Chuin, making sure your picture of Rad Rex is safe and tonight, I'll check out the white house with the iron gate."

"No," said Chiun. "We must wait for that officer. To leave now would be disrespectful to the Loni."

"How come, Chiun, these Loni have your respect?"

"Because, unlike some people, they have earned it."

"Chiun, I don't want to hurt your feelings, but really now. Every Master of Sinanju has been taught Loni dialect for centuries, because you still owe them a contract?"

"Correct."

"I kind of think that little debt might have been forgotten by now. Just how many languages do you know well?"

"Really well?"

"Yeah."

"One. My own. The rest I use."

Remo noticed an imported copy of the *New York Times* selling for $2.50. Under the fold of the front page, there was a story about the television networks adjusting their Watergate coverage to allow the showing of soap operas.

"*As the Planet Revolves* is back on the air in the states," said Remo, mildly.

"What?" demanded Chiun.

"Your shows. They're back on."

Chiun's mouth began to work as he tried to speak, but nothing came out. Finally he said, "I left America under the condition that I was leaving a void. America has lied to me. How could they have returned the programs just like that after taking them off just like that?"

"I don't know, Little Father. But I think now we can get about our business so we can get back to the States faster, right? You can pay your respects to the Loni some other time. If they've waited a couple of thousand years, they can certainly wait another one or two."

For the first time, Remo saw Chiun in conflict.

Just then, the Army captain they had spoken to walked up to them, and said, in British-tinged English: "My men and I have been delighted, sir, by your telling of that silly Loni fairy tale. To show our pleasure, we will be glad to retrieve your luggage for only one hundred dollars American."

Remo put his hand up over his mouth to stifle a laugh.

Chiun resolved his internal conflicts. The frail Oriental went whirring into the newspapers, shredding them. The stand went into a wall rack and the wall rack went into the vendor who went into the lighting fixtures along with the rack, stand and little shredded bits of white papers that slowly settled like a soft snowfall in the Busati Air Terminal.

"Just so it should not pass, this perfidy, in calmness," said Chiun. The captain who had tried to shake them down had begun to back away, when a word from Chiun stopped him.

This time, Chiun did not translate for Remo as he spoke with the captain. Finally, Chiun beckoned for Remo to follow him. As they walked behind the captain, Chiun said softly to Remo, "They are not Loni, these people."

"Good. Then let's go to the city and finish what we came to do."

"First I must finish what I came to do," Chiun said.

Several hours later, as they trudged across the Busati plain, Remo was still picking little bits of newsprint out of his jacket pockets and bitching at Chiun for deceiving him into thinking they were going back to the capital city.

"I told you," Chiun said. "An older contract takes precedence."

"That doesn't answer my problem, Little Father."

"To a fool, nothing is an answer."

"You and I are paid by the same employer. We have a job to do and we are not serving him."

"You may leave if you wish," Chiun said.

"How?" said Remo looking around the plain. "I don't even know where I am."

"When did you ever?" said Chiun and marched on happily toward the mountains in the distance. For a full day they walked and Remo complained about the assignment being missed, the Loni who would undoubtedly rob them when the two got to their village and the awesome dryness of the plain which Chiun kept referring to as the lush gardens before the mountains, for they had once, he explained, been the most beautiful gardens in the world.

"The Loni must have paid your ancestors pretty good," said Remo.

"They recognized true worth."

"They're gonna jump us as soon as we get to enough of them."

"The Loni are fair and just and decent."

"They must have really paid," said Remo. He felt clammy and dusty and grimy, not having changed clothes in two days. Chiun, naturally, had seven trunks full of changes.

As they climbed into the mountains, night descended in its awesome majesty upon the old continent. Remo noticed immediately that these were not simple paths, but stairways cut of rock worn by centuries of feet.

They continued marching into the night, pushing onward and upward. Remo was amazed at the ability of the soldiers to keep going under the burden of Chiun's baggage.

Around one bend a fire shone from a high wall.

Chiun cupped his hands to his face and yelled the Loni dialect of Swahili.

"I told them I was here," he said to Remo.

"Now we get it," said Remo, prepared to slash his way back down the mountain.

From arches in the wall came men bearing torches and spears, just a few men at first who hung back and waited until their numbers grew, and then moved forward, their torches illuminating the night with fire as though they were high beam lamps.

There were too many with too many spears to escape unscathed. Remo decided to take a route through the center, prepare his body to take some wounds, and then to keep going. Retreat was impossible. Behind him he heard Chiun's trunks striking the ground, and the scuffling feet of the Hausa soldiers as they turned and fled down the mountainside.

Oddly enough the Loni tribesmen did not pursue them. Instead, when they got within striking distance, they fell to their knees and a cry of praise rose from their throats in powerful unison.

"Sinanju. Sinanju. Sinanju."

Then, up over their heads on the mountaintop, Remo could see in the flame light, a tall black woman wearing a short white gown. She carried in her hands a shiny metal brazier from which a fire burned. Remo and Chiun moved closer, and the crowd which chanted "Sinanju" stopped, upon one word from her.

She spoke. Chiun translated for Remo.

"Welcome, Master of Sinanju. Our ambitions have been awaiting the return of your awesome magnificence. Oh, Awesome Magnificence, the Gods of the Loni greet you in fire. Our hopes await the glory of thy majestic presence. Oh, Awesome Magnificence, the throne of the Loni once again will be secure because you have deigned to come among us."

"They really saying those things about you, Chiun?" said Remo from the side of his mouth.

"That is how civilized people greet the Master of Sinanju," said Chiun, the latest Master of Sinanju.

"Shit," said Remo Williams, ex-Newark cop.

CHAPTER EIGHT

General William Forsythe Butler rented a car at the Washington, D.C. airport when his plane landed there, and drove out in the quiet night toward Norfolk, Virginia

The air was sweet with the hot smells of spring and he rode with the air conditioning turned off and the windows open, listening to the land, feeling its beauty around him.

How long ago had those first slaves set foot on this land? Had they perhaps traveled this same road? Of course, it would not have been much more than a cart path then. Perhaps the rich dirt got between their toes and warmed and welcomed them and they thought the way Butler once had: that the land was rich and good. After a trip of unrelieved brutality, perhaps they felt that they had chanced into something good—a growing, fertile land where they could build a full and rewarding life. The Loni princes would have thought that way. And instead of happiness and fulfillment, they found only the chain and the whip and the sun-hammered days of backbreaking labor in the fields, labor unrelieved by the release of humor, by the circle of family; by the slow, lazy forgetfulness of happiness.

The Loni had once been prideful people. How many

of them had tried to change their lot, first by reasoning with the white-eye brutes, then by fleeing, then by rebellion?

Butler thought of them and then of what the Loni, subjugated and beaten, had become even in their nature land.

He trod heavier on the gas pedal. In Norfolk, he drove to the city's bustling waterfront and parked his car in a now unsupervised parking lot near a small amusement arcade. Before he even left the car, the watery feel and smell of salt and brack coated everything. He could feel it working its way into the soft silk fibers of his light blue suit, as he stepped along the riverfront street.

He stopped near the piers and looked up and down the street, blinking and bright with neon lights for a half-mile in each direction. His man would be in one of three places.

The first bar was air-conditioned cold, and he felt the sweat on his body dry almost immediately as he stepped inside the door. It was a sailor's bar. A *white* sailor's bar. The tavern was filled with seamen, their clothes, their tattoos, the leathery but still untanned look of their faces and hands giving away their occupation. Heads turned toward him as he stood in the doorway, realizing he had made a mistake and this was not the bar he was looking for, but determined to brazen it out as a free man, first looking along the bar, then toward the tables, scanning faces.

"Hey, you," the bartender called. "This is a private bar."

"Yassuh," Butler said. "Jes' looking for somebody, boss."

"Well, you won't find him in here."

"Not a him, boss. A her. You see her, maybe? Big blonde woman with big titties. Wearing a little, short, red dress, way up high around the nice, fine, warm ass." He grinned, showing teeth.

The bartender sputtered.

Butler said, "Never mind, boss. She ain't here. But if she come in, you tell her to get her white ass home, 'cause her man gonna whomp her good iffen she don't. You tell her, she don't get right home, and she ain't getting no more of this good stuff right here," Butler said, stroking the groin of his trousers.

There were a few muzzled mumbles. The bartender's mouth still worked, getting ready to talk, but before he could speak, Butler turned and walked out into the street, letting the heavy wood and glass door swing shut behind him.

He stopped here on the sidewalk and laughed, a full, roaring laugh that only a trained, intelligent linguist's ear could tell was punctuated by the Loni throat click of anger.

Then Butler turned and walked away down the block. It didn't feel so oppressively hot anymore. The heat felt good on his skin.

The second tavern was uneventful, but empty and he found his man in the third saloon he entered. The man sat in the back, his face *cafe au lait* light against the dark blue of his crisp tailored gabardine uniform. Despite the heat, he wore his braided jacket and his braided duck-billed cap, with the gold stringwork across the crown and bill.

The bar was noisy with black sailors and no one looked up when Butler came in or paid any especial attention to the black dude in the light blue suit. He was twice offered drinks by sailors as he walked the length of the bar and turned them down with what he hoped was a gracious shake of his head, and finally reached the table where the ship's officer sat, drinking alone, a bottle of Cutty Sark scotch in front of him.

The officer looked up as Butler eased into the seat.

"Hello, Captain," Butler said.

"Why, Colonel Butler," the man said. "What a pleasure to see you." His tongue was a little thick in his mouth; he had been drinking too much, Butler realized with distaste. "It's been a long while."

"Yes," Butler said, "but now I have need of your services."

The ship's officer smiled softly as he filled his old-fashioned glass to the brim with Cutty Sark. He sniffed the smoky scotch, lifted it to his mouth, and then began to swallow it smoothly, slowly.

He stopped when the glass was half empty. "Why, of course," he said. "Same arrangement?"

Butler nodded.

The same arrangement meant $5,000 in cash for the captain of the Liberian-registered tanker. At least that was the polite fiction that Butler and the ship's captain maintained. The full truth was that the "same arrangement" meant that the captain's wife and mother and children who lived in Busati would continue to live there and not turn up dead in a ditch. This point had been made clear at Butler's first meeting with the captain ten months before; it had never been raised again since there was no need for it. The captain remembered.

"However," Butler added, "there will be a slight difference this time." He looked around the room to be sure no one was watching or listening. The small bar reverberated with the soul-screeching of the jukebox. Reassured, Butler said, "Two women."

"Two?" the captain said.

Butler smiled. "Two. But one will not complete the trip."

The captain sipped his drink, then smiled again. "I see," he said. "I see." But he did not see why he should carry two women for the same price he was paid for carrying one. Yet, neither did he see how he could raise the subject to Butler without risking serious trouble. Again, he said, "I see."

"Good," said Butler. "When do you sail?"

The captain glanced down at his watch. "Five o'clock," he said. "Just before dawn."

"I'll be there," Butler said. He rose from the table.

"Join me in a drink, Colonel?" the captain asked.

"Sorry, no. I never drink."

"Too bad. I should think you would. It makes life so much easier."

Butler put his big hand on the table and leaned forward to the officer. "You don't understand, Captain. Nothing could be easier than my life is now. Or more pleasurable."

The captain nodded. Butler paused a moment, almost challenging a comment, but when none came, he pushed away from the table, turned and left.

Butler's next stop was a motel on the outskirts of the city, where he rented a room under the name of F. B. Williams, producing identification in that name, paying cash and rebuffing efforts by the motel clerk to engage him in conversation.

Butler checked the room. The door locks satisfied

him. He tossed his small traveling bag on the bed and returned to the car.

For an hour, he cruised the streets of Norfolk, looking for a person. It had to be a special kind of person.

Finally, he found her. She was a tall willowy blonde with ashen hair. She stood on a corner near a traffic light in the time-honored fashion of whores everywhere—ready to cross the street if a police car came along, but willing to stand there forever if the fuzz didn't come, or at least until the right kind of man came along in the right kind of car.

Butler saw her, quickly drove the rented Buick around the block, then timed it so that he rolled up in front of her as the traffic light turned red.

The girl looked at him through the windshield and Butler pressed the button that unlocked the car doors. The heavy, clicking sound was another universal signal. The girl came over, leaned on the door and stuck her head inside the open window, carefully glancing into the back seat first. She was just about the right size and age, Butler guessed. The coloration looked about right also.

"Want to party?" she said.

"Sure," Butler said.

"Go down for $15, straight for $25."

"You go all night?" Butler asked. He thought it odd that the words and phrases of the street came back to him so easily, almost as if they had never left his mind.

"Naah," the girl said. "All night's a bummer."

"Three hundred dollars make it more pleasant?" Butler asked, knowing that the figure was outrageous and could have hired the best efforts of any three girls on the block.

"You got three hundred?"

Butler nodded.

"Let's see it."

"Get in and I'll show you."

The girl opened the door and slid into the front seat next to Butler. The light was green and he turned the corner and pulled up into a spot near an all-night bookstand.

Butler reached his wallet from his pocket and took out three one-hundred-dollar bills, making sure that the girl got a look at the remaining fat wad of bills in the wallet. He held the three up in front of the girl.

"Payment in advance," she said warily.

"Two hundred now," he said. "You can stash it. The other hundred after."

"How come you're so eager?" she said.

"Look. I'm no freak. No whips, none of that shit. I just like white women. If you're good to me, there's another hundred in it that nobody has to know about."

She looked at Butler's face again, hard this time, obviously trying to fit him into one of her danger categories of fuzz, freaks and fighters, but he didn't match. "Okay," she said, "wait here. I'm going to drop off the two hundred and I'll be right back."

Butler nodded. He wouldn't trust a prostitute out of sight for any reason but money, so he had made a point of showing her all the cash in his wallet and her little brain already was working overtime, he knew, trying to figure out how to get more out of him than the four hundred dollars already promised. She would be back as soon as she gave the two hundred to her pimp.

Three minutes later she returned and as she slid into the front seat she grabbed him.

"My name's Thelma," she said. "What's yours?"

"Simon," he said. "I've already got a room." He snapped the door locks shut and drove off.

Ten minutes later, they were in Butler's motel room. Twenty minutes later, she was tied, gagged, drugged and lying on the floor behind the bed, not visible from the window and out of reach of the telephone. The last was an unnecessary precaution because she would be out for the rest of the night.

Butler looked at her one more time before leaving the room and he was satisfied. The size was right; the hair coloring about right. It wouldn't be perfect; it certainly might not fool anyone for too long, but it should do. It would buy enough time.

He whistled as he drove out through the hot city into the rolling fox-hunting hills of rich-bitch Virginia.

He drove the road three times before he found the cutoff to the long winding drive that led to the Butler estate. With his headlights out, and after sitting in the dark for a moment, he could see the main house high up on a hill, two hundred yards from the road. He decided not to drive up; the roadway was probably hooked up to an alarm. He cruised slowly down the highway for another hundred yards, found a deep shoulder off the road covered by an overhang of trees, and drove in.

He closed the car up, checked his pockets to make sure he had his materials and then set across the razor-cut lawns of the Butler estate toward the big house on the hill, keeping close to the line of trees at the property's northern end.

As he loped, he glanced at the luminous dial of his writwatch. Cutting it close, but still enough time.

The grass oozed up a damp coolness that enveloped him as he moved, and he imagined himself in an earlier day, trudging barefooted along these hills, dressed perhaps in a monkey suit, bringing drinks to Massa on the patio. When had it happened? When had he come to hate so?

He moved in a rhythmic trot, his giant athlete's body swinging free and easy, the way he used to on the grass-covered fields of football, when he performed in the big open-air cage for the whites lucky enough to have a friend who could help them get season's tickets.

No matter when he started to hate. He hated. That was enough of an answer, but then he remembered. King Kong was why he hated.

Butler had had a particularly bitter argument with his sister, had gone out into the New York night, and somehow had wound up listening to a free lecture on racism at the New School for Social Research.

The lecturer was one of that roving band of non-teaching teachers who make a headline with one interesting, if erroneous, statement and then milk it for lecture fees at campuses for the next twenty years. The lecturer began to talk about racism in the films, drawing unsupported conclusions from unsubstantiated data, to the growing applause of the two hundred people, mostly white, in the audience.

Then the house lights dimmed and film clips from the old King Kong classic began to be shown on the screen. There were five minutes of the giant ape terrorizing Fay Wray in the jungle, then climbing the Empire State Building with her in his giant hand, then standing there atop the building until he was gunned down by the fighter planes.

The speaker seemed to want to match the auditorium darkness with the lack of light in his own analysis.

King Kong, he said, was just a thinly veiled attack by while filmmakers on black sexuality, a pandering to the redneck's fear of the potent black man. The leering expressions of King Kong as he lifted the white girl up in his giant black hand; his mindless, headlong, unswerving search for her which typified the mythical lust of black men for white women; and the cheaply symbolic end where King Kong was shot down while hanging on to the building's phallic symbol of a tower, thus signifying that the black man would be done in by his erect phallus—all these were cited as proofs by the speaker.

Butler looked around the auditorium at the heads nodding up and down in agreement.

And these were the liberals, he thought, the best hope of blacks in America—and not one of them questioned, for even a moment, their own willingness to equate a giant movie monkey with a black man. Didn't they teach anthropology in the schools any more? Didn't they teach anything? The ape was hairy, and blacks were hairless. Blacks had thick lips, but apes had no lips at all. And yet these looney-tunes could believe that people would find blacks and apes interchangeable. Why could they believe that of others, if they didn't really know it of themselves?

And *they* were supposed to be the best America had to offer.

Butler had left the auditorium convinced by the speaker of just one thing: his sister had been right and he had been wrong. *It would take confrontation and possibly violence to get what the black man deserved in America.*

Butler tried. Then came that visit to the Loni village, when William Forsythe Butler had known that he had come home. He heard the legend of the Loni and knew that he—he alone—could be the redeemer of that legend, that he could use the Loni to take over power in Busati and show what a black man could do with a government if given half a chance.

He was at the house now. It was dark and silent. He was glad there were no dogs. Willie Butler was afraid of dogs.

He paused close to the wall of the house, looking around him, remembering the floor plan that had been outlined to him by a researcher, who had found it in the Library of Congress, under Historical Homes of Virginia. The girl's room would be second floor front right.

He looked up. Latticework, buried under vines, covered the front of the big building. He hoped the thin wood would hold his weight.

Butler tested it by reaching up, grabbing a piece of wood with his right hand, and lifting his feet off the ground.

He hung there suspended by his right hand momentarily; the wood was anchored and strong. He grunted softly to himself and then began climbing the latticework like a ladder. The window to the second floor bedroom was unlocked and open slightly at the top. Inside he could hear the faint whirring of central air conditioning breathing coolness into the room.

The night was black as a railroad tunnel at midnight, and the inside of the bedroom seemed to be brightly lighted by the small lamp built into the light switch near the door.

In the bed, under a shiny sheet, he could make out a woman's form. That should be Hillary Butler.

Holding onto the latticework with one hand, Butler

inched the bottom window up until it was fully opened. Then he carefully stepped into the room, his shoes sinking deeply into the plush velvet carpet that covered the floor. He paused, sipping his breath carefully through his nose, trying to make no sound, then moved toward the bed, the foot, around the side. He could see the girl's face now. It was Hillary Butler, sleeping the dreamy sleep of the peaceful-with-the-world. That she slept in this air-conditioned room under that satin sheet because her ancestors had carted men and women and babies across an ocean in the hold of a stinking rat-infested ship, did not seem to intrude on her sleep at all. Butler hated her.

He stepped back and from his pocket took a small foil-wrapped packet. Carefully he pinched the top to break the air-tight seal.

The characteristic smell of chloroform rose from the package into his nostrils. From the packet, he pulled out a heavy gauze pad soaked with the drug, and carefully put the foil back into his jacket.

Quickly he moved forward. He stood alongside the girl and transferred the chloroform pad to his right hand. Then he reached down and covered the girl's nose and mouth with the pad. Hillary Butler bolted upright in bed, and the big man dropped his body on hers to hold her still. She thrashed for a few seconds, her eyes wide open and shocked, trying to see her attacker, but only able to see the glint of light reflecting off a golden chain-link ring on the hand that covered her face. Her thrashing slowed down. Finally, she was still.

Butler stood up and looked down at the unconscious girl. He left the pad on her face and methodically began to search the room.

He carefully went through a clothes closet that ran the length of one wall, looking at dresses and rejecting them until he found one, a blue and white jersey shift with a hand-made label from an exclusive New York City couturier. He made sure the other garments were hanging neatly before he closed the closet. On a dressing table, he saw a polished ebony wood jewelry box. He reached inside and grabbed a handful of jewelry, carried it to the room's little night light, and inspected it. He took an engraved golden charm bracelet and a pair of gem earrings. The rest he returned to the box.

Butler rolled up the blue and white dress and stuck it under the belt of his trousers. The jewelry went into an inside jacket pocket.

At the bed, he pulled the chloroform pad off the girl's face, put it back in his pocket, then lifted the girl up in one muscled arm, carrying her under his arm like a rolled up set of blueprints and went back to the window.

With ease that surprised him, he carried the girl down. Still holding her under one arm, he moved toward the line of trees and headed back for the roadway where his car waited.

He dumped the little rich girl on the floor in the back of the car, covered her with a blanket and then drove off quickly. He didn't want to be stopped by any policemen wondering what a black in a rented car was doing in this section of the county at almost three o'clock in the morning.

After parking in the motel lot in front of his room, Butler placed a fresh chloroform pad near Hillary Butler's face, then went inside his room where the prostitute was still unconscious.

He dressed her in Hillary Butler's blue and white

dress, then put on the stolen jewelry. The charm bracelet engraved on the back. "To Hillary Butler from Uncle Laurie." Earrings. They were made for pierced ears. The whore's ears were not pierced. Butler swore under his breath. Damn, just like a white bitch, not to have holes where you wanted her to. He rammed the point of one earring through the fleshy lobe of the unconscious girl who did not even stir, even though drops of blood ran down her ear from the small hole. He clipped the earring in back with the small squeeze lock attachment, then fastened the other earring in the same way.

Butler untied the girl's ropes and stashed them in his small suitcase. From a back compartment of the bag, he pulled out two heavy brown-colored plastic bags, shaped like army duffle bags.

He stuffed the prostitute into one of them. The bag locked at the top with metal snaps but there was enough gap in the closure for air to get in. General William Forsythe Butler took the other bag out into the parking lot. There was no one in sight. Only three cars were parked in the lot, and those rooms were darkened, their occupants probably asleep. Butler opened the back door of the Buick, reached in and began to feed Hillary Butler into the bag. He handled her without tenderness, breaking the strap of her light nylon nightgown. The gown slid down, revealing a creamy white well-formed breast. Butler laid his black hand on her breast, feeling its warmth, looking in the dim light at the contrast between her skin and his. He tweaked the end of the breast viciously, and the girl flinched in her stupor. He grimaced to himself as he released her. Get used to it, honey, he thought. There's gonna be more where that came from. Your family's got a three-hundred-year-old bill to pay, and payment's gonna come right out of your fine white hide.

Butler closed the bag with the snaps, then again glancing around the lot, slipped back into his room, picked up the bag containing the street girl and carried that back to the car. He tossed her into the back seat on top of Hillary Butler.

Then he cleaned everything out of the room and left, wiping all the doorknobs free of prints, and leaving the key in the door of the room.

Fifteen minutes later, his rented car was parked in a black unlit street, a scant hundred yards from the pier where the Liberian freighter was now coming to life, preparing to sail.

Butler locked the doors of his car and went looking for the captain. He found him on the bridge of the ship and whispered a few words to him.

The captain called a sailor to him and talked to him softly. "Your keys," the captain asked Butler. Butler gave them to the sailor who turned away.

Ten minutes later, he was down on dockside below the ship with a big steamer trunk on a forklift.

"Carry that trunk to my cabin," the captain told another sailor, who scurried down the gangplank and helped the other lug the heavy trunk aboard.

Butler waited a few minutes, then went to the captain's cabin.

The trunk was neatly in the middle of the floor. Butler opened it and roughly yanked the plastic bag out of the trunk. He opened the clips on top, glanced in and saw the prostitute wearing Hillary Butler's blue and white dress. Carefully, he pulled the plastic bag down until the girl's face and shoulders were free.

Butler looked around the cabin. On a small table near the captain's big bed was a fourteen-in-long bronze statuette. Butler hefted it in his hand. It was heavy enough.

He walked back and knelt alongside the unconscious whore. How peaceful she looked, he thought, as he raised the heavy statuette over his head and slammed it down with the force of a hammer into the girl's face.

Butler was thorough. He shattered her teeth, broke her facial bones, and for good measure broke one of the bones in her left arm.

He stood up, puffing slightly from the exertion. The carpet on the floor was spattered with gore, and with a towel from the captain's private bathroom, he mopped it up as best he could, then washed the statuette clean. He noted what looked like specks of blood imbedded in the link design of his gold ring, and carefully washed it out under running water.

Butler snapped the dead girl back into the bag but left it on the rug in the middle of the floor. Before leaving the room, he checked to make sure Hillary Butler was still alive in her plastic cage, then slammed the lid of the heavy trunk shut.

Back on the bridge, Butler called the captain to one side. From his inside jacket pocket, he took an envelope containing $5,000 in hundreds.

"Here," he said. "Your fee."

The captain pocketed it and then looked again at Butler with a bland open face.

"What do I do this time to earn it?"

"There is a bag on the floor of your cabin," Butler said. "When your ship is underway ten minutes and it is still dark, dump its contents overboard. It would be best if you were to do it yourself. Your crew should not know."

The captain nodded.

"And there is a trunk in your room. Inside there is another bag with another set of contents. You will follow our usual procedure with that, turning the trunk over to my man who will meet you at your next port. He will fly it to Busati."

"I see," the captain said.

Butler reached into his pocket and withdrew a half dozen of the foil packages of chloroform pads. "Take these," he said. "They may be helpful in keeping your cargo . . . let us say, pliable."

The captain stuck the packs in his pocket. "Thank you. By the way," he said, with a small smile at the corners of his mouth, "May I make use of this cargo?"

The Busati chief of staff thought a moment, thought of Hillary Butler, thought of her warm white breast, thought of her next home in the house behind the pearl door button, and shook his head. "Not this time, Captain," he said. Hillary Butler was the last one, and random rape simply would not do. There just was not enough terror in it, at least not for one whose ancestors had given his ancestors their slave name. Nothing but gang rape under his own personal supervision would suffice. For a starter.

"Sorry," he said.

The captain shrugged.

"Now don't forget with the other bag," Butler said. "Ten minutes out to sea, dump her. The current should run her ashore sometime tomorrow."

"It shall be as you say, Colonel."

"Oh, by the way, it's General now. I've been promoted."

"I'm sure you're worthy."

"I try to be," Butler said.

He took his car keys, trotted lightly down the gangplank and returned to his car. For the first time since he'd reached America, he turned his air conditioner up high.

Two hours later, he was back in the 707 jet, on his way home to Busati.

The last name on his list, he thought. The legend was coming true.

For a moment, a random thought of that American Remo and the elderly Oriental intruded on his mind, but he rejected it. By now, they would either be out of Busati or in the custody of the troops, in which case he would see that they were exiled from the country for good. The Loni legend was to be his alone to fulfill.

CHAPTER NINE

"Once we lived in palaces. Our buildings stretched to the clouds. Our land was rich and we were at peace."

The girl turned away from Remo who lay on his back on a hillock, chewing a piece of grass. "And now, this is our world," she said bitterly, waving her arm across the field of her view. "A land of thatched huts and poverty, of ignorance and disease. A land in which we are hunted by the Hausa like game animals. We are a people from whose men the courage has been bred out, like milk-giving is bred into a cow."

Remo rolled on his left side to look at the girl. She was tall and lithe, and silhouetted against the white daylight sky of Africa, she seemed blacker than was her dark skin. She wore only a short white robe in the fashion of a Grecian toga, but its outlines, too, looked dark against the hot white sky. Her back was toward Remo, and out in front of her, down at the bottom of the hill, he could see the grubby little camp which now represented the once-great Empire.

"Could be worse," Remo said.

"How?" The girl turned and came to Remo, and in a smooth graceful motion slid down to the grass alongside him. "How could it be worse for my Loni people?"

"Take my word for it," Remo said. "You complain that civilization has kind of passed your people by. Well, you haven't missed a thing. I come from what they call civilization, and I prefer it here. At least, if you stay out of the Hausas' way, you've got some kind of peace."

He reached forward and took her left hand in his. She recoiled involuntarily from him, then tried to relax, but Remo released her hand. Princesses of the Loni Empire were virgins till they were wed; they knew not of men and no man entered into them until it was by ceremony and custom ordained. His was probably the first male hand which had ever touched the beautiful artist's hand of Princess Saffah of the Loni Empire.

"Do not release me," she said. "It feels warming, your hand. And you are right, it *is* peaceful here. But peacefulness is like rain. It is nice, but always to have it pressed upon you is quite another thing."

She took Remo's hand up in hers, silent for a moment as if shocked by her own boldness. "You, for instance," she said. "You lie here now, sucking grass like a cow, and talking of how lovely peace is, and you know that as soon as you can you will go back to this world you hate."

Remo said nothing; she was right. When he found and freed the slave girls and discovered what had happened to James Forsythe Lippincott, he would leave.

"Could I stay if I wanted?" he finally said.

"I do not know. The legend is silent."

"Oh, yeah. The legend."

Since he and Chiun first had arrived two days before, they had heard of little else but the legend. Chiun had been installed, seven steamer trunks and all, in the finest thatched hut the Loni had to offer. Princess Saffah who ruled this camp as her two younger princess sisters ruled the other two Loni encampments in the nearby hills, had moved out to make room for Chiun.

"Dammit, Chiun, that's not right," Remo had said. "Move into some other place instead of moving people around."

"Not right?" Chiun said. "What is not right? That the people of the Loni should not honor a man who has come thousands of miles across the seas to repay a debt centuries old and to put them back into power? They should not give up a hut to a man who will give them palaces?"

"Yeah, but moving their princess?"

"Princess? Suddenly you are a royalist. Remember this then. Princesses and princes and kings and queens come and go. But there is only one Master of Sinanju."

"Talk about the world being lucky," Remo said sarcastically.

"Yes, the world is lucky to have such a one. But even luckier are you who have been permitted to bask in the warmth of the Master's magnificence."

And so Chiun had moved into the hut of Princess Saffah.

In quiet protest, however, Remo refused. He insisted upon moving into one of the smaller huts of the village. The first night he was cold. The second night he was wet. The morning of the third day, he walked into Chiun's hut with his blanket in his hand.

"I thought you might be lonely," Remo said, "so I decided to move in to keep you company."

"I am happy you think so much of me," Chiun said. "But please, I would not want you to do anything against your principles."

"No, that's all right, Chiun. I've made my mind up. I'll stay."

"No," Chiun said. "I insist."

"Sorry, Chiun, I'm not leaving. I'm going to stay here and keep you company whether you like it or not."

"You are leaving this instant," Chiun said, and then called the entire Loni village to remove Remo by force if necessary. As Remo slunk away back to his own little mud hut, he could hear Chiun explaining behind him: "Sometimes the child forgets himself and must be reminded of his place. But he is young and will yet learn."

Remo had wandered up the hill and Princess Saffah had followed him. She had come to console him.

"Yeah, the legend," Remo repeated. "Look, you're a smart girl. Do you really believe the Loni are going to return to power because Chiun is here?"

"Not just the Little Father," she said. "You are here too and you are part of the legend." She opened the palm of his hand and pretended to examine it. "Tell me, when did you die?" She laughed as she felt Remo's hand tense momentarily. "You see," she said laughing. "The legend speaks only truth."

"You'd better tell me of this legend," Remo said. He was happy that she still clung to his hand.

"Once," she began, "many years ago there was a Master from across the sea. And because he stood with the Loni, the Loni were a great and just people. They lived in peace; they inflicted injustice upon no man. In the ancient days, by your calendar, the great libraries of the world were said to be at Alexandria in the land of Egypt. But the greatest of all was at Timbuktu and it was the library of the Loni. This is true, what I am telling you, Remo, you could look it up. And it was the

Loni Empire that gave to the world the gift of iron. That, too, is true. We had men who could repair damaged eyes; we had physicians who could heal those with twisted brains; all these things, the Loni had and did and we were a great people, blessed of God.

"It was said of the Master that the Loni had given him their courage for safekeeping, while they used their heads for science and their hands for art. And then this Master from across the sea went away and the Loni who had relied on him were overwhelmed by an inferior people and our empire was lost. Our best men and women were sold into slavery. We were hunted and tracked like animals until we retreated, three small bands all that was left, into these hills where you now find us and where we hide from our enemies.

"But this Master sent word across the years and across the seas and across the mountains that one day he would return. He would bring with him a man who walked in the shoes of death, a man whose earlier life had ended, and this man would face in mortal combat an evil man who would keep the Loni in chains. That is you, Remo, and this is truth I tell you."

Remo looked up and saw that Princess Saffah's dark eyes were tinged with sadness.

"Does the legend say whether I win or lose the fight?" Remo asked.

"No," she said. "The legend is silent. But it tells what must happen. The Loni children must come home. And if you are victorious, the Lonis will again rule the land and children will be able to walk the streets and the blind again can be made to see."

"It sounds like I'm doing all the work," Remo said. "What does the legend say of Chiun? Does he do anything except lay in your hut down there like Henry the Eighth?"

Princess Saffah laughed, and the smile brought beauty back to her finely chiseled face. "You must not speak unkindly of the Little Father. Centuries of hardship have changed the Loni people. Where once we were kind, we are now vindictive. Where once we had charity, we now have malice; where love, now hate; where courage, now cowardice. It is written that the Master will purify the Loni people in the ritual of the sacred fire. In that fire, he will restore to the Lonis the goodness that once was theirs, so that they may again be fit to rule this land. The Little Father may perish in this task, which is why we revere him so."

Remo rolled over and searched Saffah's deep eyes. "Perish?"

"Yes. So it is written. The flames may consume him. He is a very great man to come back to us, knowing that here he may hear the clock strike the hour of his death."

"Chiun knows this?"

"Of course," Saffah said. "He is the Master, is he not? Did you not hear his words when first he arrived? No, of course not, you would not understand because he spoke the tongue of the Loni. But he said, 'I have traveled these ages from the land of Sinanju to stand here again with my brothers, the Loni, and to place my body on the sacred coals to purify their lives with my life.' "

"He didn't tell me," Remo said. "He didn't say anything about any ritual fire."

"He loves you very much," the princess said. "He would not worry you."

"What about you, Saffah? You believe the legend?"

"I must, Remo. I am first in the line of succession to

the crown of the Loni Empire. My faith sustains my people's faith. Yes. I believe. I have always believed. I have believed in the past when others have come to us and we thought, perhaps *here,* perhaps *this* is the redeemer of the legend. But when they failed, it was just their failure, not the failure of the legend. Not long ago, another came and we believed that he might be the one but now, now that you and the Little Father have arrived, we know that he was not the one. You are."

"We who are about to die salute you," Remo said.

She leaned forward and said closely to his face. "Do you believe in sin, Remo?"

"I don't think anything is wrong between two consenting orangutans."

"I do not understand." Her face assumed a look of quizzicality which softened when she saw Remo smile. "You jest," she accused. "You jest. Someday you must tell me of your jesting and what it means."

"I will someday," he said. "No, I don't believe too much in sin. I think sin is not being able to do your job. Not much else."

"I am glad you have said that, because it is said to be a sin for a Princess of the Loni to know a man before she is wed. And yet, Remo, I want to know you and I want you to enter into me."

"Best offer I've had today," Remo said lightly, "but I think you ought to think about it some more."

Princess Saffah leaned forward, pressed her lips against Remo's and kissed him hard. She pulled her head back triumphantly. "There," she said. "I have already committed the sin of touching a man. Now when your time comes, you will have no reason not to take me."

"When I'm sure you're ready," Remo said, "no reason could have stopped me. But first duty calls."

Duty for Remo meant two things: freeing the girls in the white house behind the iron gate and finding out what had happened to Lippincott.

But Princess Saffah could give him no answers to either of those problems, although she suggested that if evil was involved, it was probably the work of General Obode.

"We have a friend," she said, "in Obode's camp. Perhaps he will be able to help you."

"What's his name?" Remo asked.

"He is a countryman of yours," Saffah said. "His name is Butler."

CHAPTES TEN

In the American circles that concerned themselves with the activities of the Four Hundred, it was well known that the Forsythes and the Butlers talked only to their cousins, the Lippincotts, and that the Lippincotts talked only to God or to whomever else could match His credentials.

So when the body washed onto the beach a few miles from Norfolk, Virginia, pummeled and battered by the stones near the shore, it became a big story because the body was identified as that of Hillary Butler. The identification was made through her blue-and-white dress and from engraved jewelry the corpse wore.

The Butler family bit its lip, as such families do, and refused to indulge in speculation for the press as to how their daughter, soon to be married, had managed to wind up dead and drowned in the ocean.

The family detested the whole idea, but part of the routine in such accidental deaths was an autopsy.

Clyde Butler was called by the county medical examiner that afternoon.

"Mr. Butler, I have to see you," the doctor said.

Resentfully, Butler agreed and made an appointment to see the examiner at his private medical office, where

Butler's arrival would not draw attention, as it certainly would have at the county administration building.

Despite the unseasonable spring heat, Butler wore a heavy dark pin-striped suit as he sat in the doctor's office, facing him across a tan-painted metallic desk.

"I suppose it's about my poor daughter," Butler said. "Really, haven't we gone through enough without. . .?"

"That's just it, sir," the doctor said. "That body was not your daughter's."

Butler could not speak. Finally, he said, "Repeat that."

"Certainly. The dead girl who washed ashore was not your daughter."

"You're sure of this?"

"Yes, sir. In making the autopsy, I discovered that the girl whose body was found had syphilis. Discreetly, I obtained your family's records from your physician and dentist. It was very difficult because of the mutiliation, but I can now say without a twinge of doubt that some other young woman is on the slab at the morgue right now."

Butler grimaced at what he considered unnecessarily explicit phrasing by the doctor.

He thought momentarily, then said: "Have you told anyone else?"

"No one at all. I wanted to talk to you first. Frankly, I did not know if your daughter might have known this other girl, or if your daughter's disappearance might be tied in somehow with this girl's death, or precisely what. It's only fair to tell you that the dead girl wasn't drowned. She was dead before she entered the water. I thought before I announced anything I would give you a chance to explain."

"You've done very well," Butler said, "and I appreciate your thoughtfulness. I would like you to do something else for me, if you would."

"If I can."

"Give me an hour and then I will be back here. Then we can decide what to do and what to say."

"Of course, Mr. Butler. Just so long as we both understand that I must fulfill the requirements of my office."

"Naturally I understand that, Doctor. Just an hour."

Butler left the doctor's office. In the middle of the next block was a bank in which the Butler family was the controlling stockholder. Butler went in, spoke briefly to the bank president, and in five minutes was ensconced, as he had asked to be, in a private office with a private telephone and a guarantee of no interruptions.

It was a sticky problem, Butler realized. At first blush, he would immediately think kidnaping and ransom. But why then would the kidnapers have gone to the trouble of dressing someone in Hillary's clothes and jewelry and trying to make it appear as if his daughter were dead? No. Kidnaping was out. Therefore, the next step might be that Hillary herself was somehow involved in this. He had no idea how to handle a thing like that, no knowledge of police processes. And hanging over it all was the publicity problem because of the Butler family's relationship with the Lippincotts.

Children with a problem go to their fathers. Butler went to the head of the Lippincott family and all its branches, Laurence Butler Lippincott.

Succinctly, calmly, he told Lippincott over the phone what had happened. Lippincott, with no trace of emotion in his voice, got Butler's number and told him to stay put; he would call him back.

From Laurence Butler Lippincott, a call went to the Senate Office Building. From there, a call went to the White House. From the White House, a special call went to Folcroft Sanitarium in Rye, New York. Problems were discussed, options were considered, decisions were reached.

The links in the chain were then reversed, and finally, the telephone rang in the air-conditioned bank office where Butler sat.

"Yes," he said.

"This is Laurie. Please listen very carefully. We believe your daughter is alive, but that she is no longer in this country. The very highest agencies in our government are now attempting to rescue her. This rescue effort, however, is guaranteed to fail if the people involved suspect that we know anything except what they wanted us to think. Therefore this is what we will do."

Butler listened as Laurie Lippincott spoke. Finally he said, "What of Martha?" thinking of his wife who was in a state of near collapse.

"She's already done the worst of her suffering," Lippincott said. "Tell her nothing."

"Nothing? But she ought to know."

"Why? So she can worry? Become hysterical? Perhaps drop a word here or there that could mean Hillary's death? Please. The very best thing is to let her think Hillary is dead. If we can get Hillary back, Martha can rejoice. And if we fail, well, one can only grieve once."

"What are the chances, Laurie?"

"I won't lie to you. They're less than fifty-fifty. But we're pulling out every stop. The best we have is on it."

"We? You mean the family?"

"No. I mean the United States of America," Lippincott said.

Butler sighed. "Okay, Laurie. Whatever you say. But I'm worried about the doctor. He's a snotty young bastard. He may give me flak."

Laurence Butler Lippincott took the name of the doctor, while allowing himself a small chuckle. "He shouldn't be too difficult," he said. Not if his tax return is like most doctors'."

So it was that ten minutes later, Butler was back in the office of the doctor, explaining that the doctor must remain silent, must permit the funeral to go ahead as if the dead body were really that of Hillary Butler.

"Never," the doctor said angrily. "I don't know what your game is, but I'm not playing it."

His intercom rang. The doctor picked up the phone and said sharply, "I said I wasn't to be . . . oh . . . oh, I see. Yes, of course."

He pressed a blinking lit button on the telephone receiver. Warily, he said, "This is he." He said nothing else for a full sixty seconds. Finally, he said, "Of course, Senator. Yes. Senator, I understand. Of course. No problem. Be glad to, Senator. Yes, I understand." When he hung up the phone, beads of perspiration dotted his forehead.

He looked at Butler and nodded. "I won't say a thing," he said.

"Good," Butler said. "Sometime in the near future, I hope to be able to explain all this to your satisfaction," he added, wondering if he were not making too big a concession to a social inferior.

The doctor raised a hand. "No need of that. Whatever you want."

"Then, good day," Butler said. "I must go to the funeral home and console my wife."

In Rye, New York, Dr. Harold W. Smith leafed through a pile of reports and tried not to think of the Butler girl or of Remo and Chiun, five thousand miles away in Busati.

He had done the best he could and assigned his top weapons to the project. There was nothing more he could do, so there was no point in worrying.

Right? Wrong. Unless the matter were cleared up satisfactorily there might be substantial problems coming from the direction of the Lippincott family. And if they leaned into the President, the President might just fall over on top of Smith, Remo, Chiun and the whole CURE operation.

And the Lippincotts wouldn't give a damn that Smith had been considering America's best interests when he told Remo he could not kill General Obode.

Unless Remo moved pretty quickly, the whole mess might be beyond unscrambling.

He wished Remo would phone, but he knew it was not likely. It took forever for CURE's Busati source to reach them by telephone, and he was a high official of the government. Smith thought of the CURE contact, ex-CIA man William Forsythe Butler. Perhaps if Remo were not successful in getting this squared away quickly, Smith might contact Butler for his advice and help.

CHAPTER ELEVEN

The man trotting up the hill wore immaculate white gabardines cut in the style of a British khaki bush uniform.

As he walked into the village, he called aloud a few words of the guttural Loni tongue. The village at first seemed deserted, but slowly people came out of huts and greeted him.

General William Forsythe Butler stood in the center court of all the huts, talking to Loni tribesmen, scanning the village, looking for a glimpse of Princess Saffah.

She came around a corner and his face lit when he saw her.

"Oh, Butleh," she said, "we are glad you have returned to visit your people."

He reached for her, then withdrew his hands. He wanted to tell her of Hillary Butler, but held back. Perhaps she would not share his view that the act of revenge had helped even more to cast him in the mold of the Lonis' redeemer.

"I am glad to be here," he said.

"We have great news." To his raised eyebrow, she said, "Yes. The legend. It is being fulfilled."

She knew, Butler thought, but how had she guessed? It didn't matter. It was enough that Saffah and the rest of the Loni knew the legend was being fulfilled in his person. He smiled to her, the warm knowing smile that one smiled to another with whom he shared a secret.

He would have preferred it another way. It would have been better if he and Saffah had been able to discuss it first and then announce it to the Loni in the proper fashion. But if this was the way it was to be, well, who was he to argue? One must seize the moment of history; time is not always tidy.

Graciousness would probably be the right approach, so he smiled at Saffah, a smile of acceptance that said there would always be between them a special bond of friendship.

She smiled back, the smile a teacher gives a student who has not thrown up on his desk that day, then turned and extended an arm toward the hut Butler knew was hers.

The entrance to the hut was empty, and then framed in the doorway, wearing a yellow robe stood the small Oriental of the hotel and the airport.

He stood there benignly, his arms folded in front of him.

"Sinanju," the villagers cried as if in one voice.

"Sinanju."

The old man smiled and raised his arms for silence, with all the sincerity of Jack Paar trying to quiet the opening applause.

Saffah turned back to Butler. "He is the Master for whom we have waited. He has come these many miles across the seas. The legend comes true."

"But . . . but . . . but what of the man who gave up his life?" Butler asked.

Just then, Chiun stepped aside and Remo came out of the hut. He saw Butler, nodded a greeting, and then snapped his fingers.

"I got it now," he said. "Willie. Willie Butler. I saw you against the Packers one day at the Stadium. I've been trying to place you since the first time I met you. Well, I'll be . . . old Willie Butler." He advanced toward Butler as if to shake his hand, but General William Forsythe Butler turned on his heel and walked away, trying to put distance between himself and the memory of the Willie Butler who once was an entertainer of white men.

By dinnertime, Butler had regained his composure and begun to make his plans. When his men had told him they had found no trace of the American and the Oriental, he had thought they had left the country. But they were here now, and so a new plan had to be set up. There had been fulfillments of the legend before, and they had turned out false. And so it would be again. When Remo and Chiun were dead, the Loni would recognize that only in Butler was the legend come to life.

Butler ate with Saffah, Chiun and Remo, in the large hut which Chiun had taken over. They sat on reed mats around a rock slab table that reflected the scarceness of hardwood in their barren hilly empire, and ate the flesh of fowl.

"You have come from Sinanju?" Butler asked.

Chiun nodded.

"Why?"

"Because there is a debt owed to the people of the Loni. A debt unpaid is an affront to my ancestors."

"So you will restore the Loni to power? How?"

"As it is written. In the purifying rites of the fire." Chiun ate delicately, then wiped his mouth with a silken cloth from one of his streamer trunks.

"And you?" Butler said to Remo.

"Me? I'm the man who accompanied Chiun to Loni-land. Just a second banana. Tell me, you ever hear of a white house behind an iron gate?"

Butler hesitated. Of course. A U.S. agent, come to solve the mystery of the girls.

"Why?" he asked.

"Because I understand there's something there I ought to see."

"There is such a house," Butler said. "But it is under the personal protection of General Obode," he added, repeating the lie he had told to his CURE contact.

"His house?" Remo asked.

Butler nodded. "He is a man of curious tastes." A plan was beginning to form in his mind.

"I want to see it," Remo said.

"I can tell you where it is, but I cannot take you there," Butler said. "Being discovered would put an end to my career with Obode and I need that career to help my Loni people."

"You a Loni?" Remo asked. "A Loni from Morgan State? You're probably the only guy in the tribe who ever played cornerback. Old Willie Butler."

"The location of the house is in the capital city of Busati," Butler said coldly. "From my sources, I know that it is guarded. It will be very dangerous."

He gave Remo the location of the building. "We'll be careful," Remo said.

Butler nodded. "One can never be too careful in this land."

It was agreed Remo and Chiun would visit the house before dawn. Butler left the camp shortly after dinner, on the pretext that important business awaited his return to Busati.

But the only business on his mind was the warning he wanted to give General Obode about the two imperialist American agents who were planning to assassinate him, but who would be vulnerable tonight because Butler had enticed them into visiting his house of many pleasures.

CHAPTER TWELVE

In an American city, it would have been a ghetto, a slum, the final demonstration that capitalism could not work unless it allowed the hog robber-baron rich to step on the poor man's neck and grind his face into the dirt.

But in Busati, it was one of the better streets. And the whorehouse behind the iron gate was definitely one of the better buildings.

It had once belonged to a British general who had come to the country planning to teach the heathen savages a thing or two, and who had instantly developed a letch for black women of all sizes and shapes. He had had his throat slit one night by a woman whom he thought loved him for his obviously superior soul.

She took his wallet and the seventy-three British pound notes it contained and returned to her native village where she was as venerated as Marjorie Meriwether Post.

The house meanwhile was recaptured by the Busati government for non-payment of the four-dollar annual real estate tax—Busati facing its own urban crisis at the time, the necessity to buy another four push-brooms for the one-man street cleaning force who was charged with keeping the city immaculate.

The house had since that time belonged to the Busati government, remaining vacant until now-General William Forsythe Butler took it over and decided to use it for his own purposes.

"Look. In the tree," Chiun said. "Have you ever seen such foolishness?"

In the dark, Remo's eyes made out the figure of a soldier with a gun, notched in the fork of the tree across the street from the white house.

"And in the window of that building over there," Remo said softly, gesturing with his eyes toward the window whre he had just seen a glint of light that could come only from a rifle barrel. "It looks as if General Obode is expecting company tonight."

Remo and Chiun stood in the shadows, half a block away from the large white house behind the metal gate.

"And look," Chiun said, "there are two . . . no, three more behind that motor vehicle over there."

"I guess no one told them that the Master of Sinanju was coming," Remo said. "They're not properly impressed."

"We must do our best to remind them of their good manners," the old man said.

Before Remo could say a word in answer, Chiun was up at the large stone wall. His fingers bought a hold in the wall and he smoothly clambered up it, paused momentarily on the top and then vanished into the grounds behind the fourteen-foot-high barrier.

Remo moved close to the wall and heard Chiun say, "Shall I send a litter bearer for you, my son?"

"Up yours, My Father," Remo said, but too softly for Chiun to hear. Then Remo, too, was up and over the stone wall.

He stood alongside Chiun. "Better be careful," he said. "There are probably more soldiers in here."

"Oh, thank, you, Remo," Chiun said.

"For what?"

"For alerting me to danger. For helping to prevent me from falling asleep and into the hand of these terrible dangerous men. Oh me, oh my." This was Chiun's new phrase which he had picked up from Rad Rex on the last installment he had seen of *As the Planet Revolves,* the one show, Remo swore, in all of television history in which nothing not only never happened, but in which nothing even threatened to happen.

"Buck up, Chiun," Remo hissed. "The only thing we have to fear is fear itself. I'll protect you."

"My heart soars like the eagle."

They moved through the darkness toward the house. "Are you sure," Chiun said, "that this is what you want to do?"

"It's what I was supposed to do before you tricked me into playing Prince Charming for that gang on the mountain," Remo said.

"Please not to embarrass me," Chiun said. "The Loni might hear of any foolishnesses of yours and this would lower me in their eyes." Chiun led the way up one of the stone walls of the house and into an open second-floor window. The room they entered was empty; they moved out into a broad dimly-lit hallway, built like a balcony, from which they could see the main door of the house below.

Behind the door were a half-dozen soldiers wearing Busati whites and carrying American Army grease guns. One of the soldiers was a sergeant. He looked at his watch.

"Very soon now," he said. "Very soon we will have our company and we will put them to sleep."

"Good," one of the privates said. "I hope they come quickly so we have time to sample the merchandise."

"By all means," the sergeant said. "This merchandise is to be sampled as often as possible, as vigorously as necessary. *Mi casa est su casa.*"

"What does that mean?" the first soldier asked.

"That means screw your brains out," another soldier said. "Use up that white ass."

"I can hardly wait," the first soldier said. "Where are those bastards anyway?"

"Right here," Remo said. He stood on the balcony looking down toward the main entrance. At his side stood the tiny Chiun, wearing not his customary robe, but a black Ninja costume which he wore only at night.

"I said, right here, you stupid gorilla bastard," Remo said, louder this time.

Chiun shook his head. "Always on display," he said. "Do you never learn?"

"I don't know, Chiun. Something about him there just pisses me off."

"Hey, you, get down out of there." The sergeant spoke.

"Come and get us," Remo said. "Use the stairs. They work both ways."

"You come down from there or, by God, we're gonna plug you."

"You're all under arrest," Remo said, seeing himself as Cary Grant in the temple of the thugs.

Chiun leaned against the railing, shaking his head in disgust.

The sergeant started for the stairs, followed by the

other five soldiers. They moved slowly and Remo wondered why.

"Oh, oh," Remo said. "I just thought. If they fire their guns, the guys outside'll hear it and come in," Remo whispered to Chiun.

"I doubt much that you 'just thought' of anything," Chiun said, "since you seem incapable of thought. But if that worries you, don't let them fire guns," Chiun said as if that answered everything.

"Of course," Remo said. "Why didn't I think of that? Don't let those six men fire their guns."

"Not six. Ten," a voice said from behind Remo. He turned. Standing in an open doorway was another soldier in Busati whites. He carried an automatic. Behind him in the dimness, Remo could see three more men. He realized now why the sergeant had been very slow about leading his men upstairs; he was waiting for the other half of the trap to close.

"I surrender," Remo said, raising his hands.

"A wise decision, friend," the soldier with the automatic said. He nodded to the other three men who poured out of the room and joined the six men coming up the stairs. They put their guns away, slinging them back over their chests, as they surrounded Remo and the small Korean.

After all, ten against two did not require weapons, did they?

Of course not.

The sergeant, who was the house doorman, as much as told them that before he felt himself being lifted up by the small Oriental, and then being spun around as if he were a long stick and used as a battering ram against the other men.

The soldier who had been in the doorway reached for his automatic again to free it from the holster.

But the holster was gone, ripped away from his side by the young American. "This yours?" Remo said. Stupidly, the soldier nodded. Remo gave them back. Holster, automatic and ammunition right through the soldier's face into his throat. Deep.

Behind him, Remo heard the thwack, thwack, thwack, the machinelike periodicity that meant Chiun was at work.

"Chiun, keep one of them alive," Remo yelled, before two soldiers were on him. Then he violated his own injunction, dropping them heavily onto the body of the soldier whose face had sprouted a gun.

Then there were no more sounds. Remo turned to Chiun who was releasing the feet of the sergeant he had used as a battering ram. The soldier slipped shapelessly onto a pile of bodies.

"Chiun, dammit, I said . . ."

Chiun raised a hand. "This one breathes," he said. "Therefore present your lectures to someone who needs them. Perhaps you might talk to yourself."

The sergeant groaned and Remo reached down and yanked him roughly to his feet.

"The girls," Remo said. "Where are they?"

The sergeant shook his head to clear it. "All this for women?"

"Where are they?" Remo said.

"The room at the end of the hall."

"Show us."

Remo shoved the sergeant who led the way down the wide oak-planked hallway, staggering slightly from side to side. A head wound dripped blood onto his white uniform. His right arm hung limply; a shoulder separation, Remo thought. He grabbed the sergeant's right wrist and yanked, then choked off the sergeant's scream by tossing his hand around the soldier's mouth.

"Just a reminder," Remo growled, "that we ain't your friendly neighborhood team of United Nations advisors. No tricks."

The sergeant, his eyes wide with fright and pain, nodded quickly, almost frantically.

He walked faster, then stopped outside a large oak door at the end of the hall. "In there," he said.

"You first."

The sergeant unlocked the door with a key from a ring on his belt, pushed open the door and stepped inside.

The room was just beginning to be lit by the first dim blush of the morning sun. Remo forced the pupils of his eyes to wide, and in the darkness, he could see four bunks. Each was occupied.

The four women in the beds were naked. They were tied with ropes, their arms up over their heads lashed to the bed posts. Their legs pulled wide apart and their ankles tied to the posts at the foot of the beds. Cloth gags were in their mouths.

In the faint glints of light from the window and from the hallway, their eyes sparkled as they watched Remo. They looked like animals peering from the dark ring around a campfire.

The room smelled of excrement and sweat. Remo brushed past the sergeant and entered the room. The sergeant looked around but Chiun stood in the doorway behind him, blocking escape.

Remo took the gag from the girl in the nearest bunk

and as he did leaned forward close enough to see her clearly. Her face was scarred and broken. One eye had been deformed from a badly healed beating. Her mouth was toothless.

Whip marks covered her naked front from her face to her ankles. Hard black cankers dotted her body where it had been used as an ashtray.

Remo released the gag and said, "Don't worry. We're friends. You're going to be all right now."

"Be all right," she repeated dully. She smiled suddenly, the toothless grimace of an old hag. Her eyes sparkled. "Treat you nice, mister. You like to whip me? I do everything if you whip me. Hard. You like hard? I like hard. Make me bleed, I treat you nice, mister. You like kiss me?" She puckered up her mouth and scroontched an imaginary kiss toward Remo.

He shook his head and backed away from her.

"Hee, hee, hee," the vision cackled. "I got money. I treat you right if you whip me hard. My family is rich. I pay. Just hit me, soldier boy."

Remo turned away. He went to two more girls. They were the same. Lamed, twisted, mindless husks that once were people. None of them could have been much over twenty, but they spoke with the grim sadness of ancient wizened women who sit on corners and whose eyes suddenly light up as they remember something nice that once happened to them. Nice was, for these girls, the whip, the chain, the knife, the extinguished cigarette.

The fourth girl began to cry when Remo removed her gag. "Thank God," she said. "Thank God for somebody."

"Who are you?" Remo asked.

Through her tears and sobbing, she said, "I'm Hillary

Butler. They kidnaped me. I've been here two days."

"Kinda rough, kid, huh?"

"Please," she said. Remo began to free her.

Behind him, he heard the sergeant start to speak. "I have nothing to do with it, man," but his words were cut off as he oomphed, Chiun putting a hard hand into his back.

"Who are these others?" Remo asked, as he tore the knots from Hillary Butler's ropes.

"I don't know," she said. "Americans too, the sergeant said. But there's nothing much left of them. They're on heroin."

"You too?" Remo asked.

"Just twice," the girl said. "Last night was the first time, and then this morning."

"You may be all right then," Remo said. "It doesn't work that way."

"I know." The girl stood up and then suddenly put her bare arms around Remo and began to sob heavily. "I know," she blubbered. "I've been praying. And I knew when I stopped praying that it would be all over. I'd be just like them."

"It's okay now," Remo said. "We got here in time. At least for you." He led her to a closet where robes hung and covered her uncut naked body with one. "Can you walk?" he asked.

"Just bruised but unbroken," she said.

Remo's voice grew hard and cold. "Chiun, take Miss Butler downstairs and wait for me. You," he said to the sergeant.

"Get in here."

Reluctantly, the sergeant entered the room. Remo

closed the door behind him, after watching Chiun lead Hillary Butler down the hallway.

"How long have these girls been here?" Remo asked.

"Different times," the sergeant said. "Three months. Seven months."

"You give them the narcotics?"

The sergeant looked toward the closed door. He looked toward the window where the sky was brightening with the pre-dawn sun rays.

"Answer me," Remo said.

"Yes, boss. I give them. They die now without them."

"There was a man named Lippincott who came here. Where is he?"

"Dead. He killed one of the girls. She recognized him, probably. So he got killed too."

"Why all the soldiers here tonight?"

"General Obode put the guard here. He expected someone to break in. Must have meant you. Look, I got some money. If you let me go, it's yours."

Remo shook his head.

The sergeant's eyes brightened. "You like the girls, mister? They take good care of you. I housebreak them well. Anything you want, they do." His voice came faster now. It pleaded even though the words themselves were not a plea. Not yet.

Remo shook his head.

"You going to kill me, man?"

"Yes."

The sergeant lunged at Remo. Remo waited; he let the sergeant grab his arm; he allowed the sergeant to hit him with a punch. He wanted to put meaning into what he was about to do, and the best way was to remind himself that this was a man. Let him touch, let him feel, let him understand what was coming.

Remo waited, then jammed his left fingertips forward into the sergeant's separated right shoulder. The sergeant stopped as if suddenly simonized in place.

Remo hit again in the same spot with his left fingertips, then with his right, then with his left again, hammering shot after shot into precisely the same place. The sergeant swooned and fell to the floor. Remo kneeled down over him, grabbed a handful of neck and twisted. The sergeant came awake, his eyes staring at Remo in horror and fright, glinting, Remo realized suddenly, like the eyes from the beds, watching the tableau.

"Awake now?" Remo said. "Good."

He lunged forward again into the injured shoulder. Beneath his fingertips he could feel the once strong and stringy muscles and fibers turning into soft mush. Still his fingertips pounded. The softer the target became, the harder Remo struck. The sergeant was unconscious now, long past reviving. Remo wished he could think of something more painful. The cloth around the sergeant's shoulder was ripped now and pummeled into powder. Remo kept hitting. Blood and ooze and chips of bone came out under his fingertips. The skin had long since given way.

Remo reared back and came forward one last time. His right fingertips went through where once there had been cloth and skin and muscle and flesh and bone. The fingertips came to rest on the wooden floor.

His anger spent, Remo stood. He kicked the sergeant's right arm away. It rolled awkwardly like an imperfect log, finally coming to rest under the bed Hillary Butler had vacated. Then Remo came down on the sergeant's face with both feet, feeling the crunch and crack beneath him. He stood, looking down at the sergeant, realizing that he had taken out of him a payment in advance for what Remo still must do. The three women, still tied in their beds, looked at Remo wordlessly.

He moved to them one after another, sitting on the edges of their beds. To each one he whispered, "Dream happy dreams," and then as gently and painlessly as he could, he did what he had to do.

Finally he was done. He untied the hands and feet of the three dead girls and covered their bodies with robes from the closet. Then he walked out into the hallway and closed the door behind him.

The instructions from Smith had been to keep Obode alive. Well, Smith could take his instructions and shove them. If Obode got anywhere in Remo's way, if he got within his line of vision, if he came anywhere within reach, Obode would know pain such as he had never even guessed existed. When Remo was done with him, he would consider the sergeant in the girls' room blessed.

Chiun waited at the foot of the steps with Hillary Butler. She looked at Remo. "The others?" she said.

Remo shook his head with finality. "Let's go," he said evenly.

Already, Smith would go berserk because Remo had not freed the other three girls. But Smith had not been there, had not seen them. Remo *had* freed them, the only way they could be freed. It had been his decision and he had made it. Smith had nothing to say about it, just as he no longer had anything to say about what Remo would do to Obode if the chance presented itself.

Only two soldiers guarded the back of the building through which Chiun and Remo exited.

"I'll take them," Remo said.

"No, my son," Chiun answered. "Your anger breeds danger for you. Protect the child."

The sun was almost rising. Remo saw Chiun and then in a flash, saw him no longer as the little man in the black costume of the Ninja night devils slid away into what was left of the darkness.

From his position inside the back doorway of the house, Remo could see the soldiers clearly, twenty-five feet away at the base of a tree. But he never saw Chiun. Then he saw the two soldiers, still there, but suddenly their bodies were twisted, useless. Two corpses. Remo strained his eyes. Still no sign of Chiun. Then, Chiun was in front of him.

"We go."

Two blocks from the house, an Army jeep was parked at the curb with a soldier behind the wheel.

Remo came up behind him. "Taxi," he said.

"This is no taxi," the soldier said, wheeling and staring angrily at Remo.

Remo extended his bloodied hands toward the soldier.

"Too bad, Charley, cause that was your only chance."

Remo left the soldier's body lying in the street and helped Hillary Butler into the back where Chiun sat alongside her.

Remo started the motor and peeled rubber, burning off down the pockholed dirt street, heading for the hills over which the sun was now rising in its daily ritual of the affirmation of life.

CHAPTER THIRTEEN

"How many are dead?" Obode's question was an elephantine trumpet.

"Thirteen," General William Forsythe Butler said.

"You said there were only two men coming."

"That's all there were."

"They must be very special men," Obode said.

"They are, Mr. President. One comes from the East; the other is an American. Already, the Loni talk that they are the fulfillment of the legend."

Obode slumped down in his velvet-backed chair in the big Presidential office.

"So they come to restore the Loni to power by grinding into dust the man of evil."

"That's what the legend says," Butler said.

"I have tolerated the Loni and their legend long enough. I was wrong, Butler, to listen to you, to try to bring the Loni into the government. Now, Dada is going to do what he should have done before. I am going to wipe out that accursed tribe."

Butler lowered his eyes so that Obode would not see the exultation there. Let him think Butler looked away to hide his disagreement. But now that the cursed Oriental and American had escaped the trap, this was best. Let Obode chase them; let Obode kill them; and then Butler would take care of Obode. Men loyal to him were now in positions of power throughout the government; they would flock to Butler's support. The Loni would acclaim him as the man who embodied the legend, and with a united country, Butler could return Busati to the power and dignity it held centuries before.

"Shall I mobilize the Army?" Butler asked.

"The Army? For the Loni? And for two men?"

"Those two men just killed thirteen," Butler protested.

"Yes. But they did not face Big Daddy. And they did not face you, Butler. One company and us. That will be enough to take care of both the Loni and the legend, once and for all."

"You have tried before to eliminate the Loni," Butler reminded him.

"Yes. Back before you arrived here. And always they scurried, like bugs before heat. And then I stopped because I listened to you. But this time, I will not stop and I do not think the Loni will run." He grinned a broad faceful of mirth. "After all, are not the redeemers of the legend there among them?"

Butler nodded. "So it is said."

"Well, we shall see, Butler."

Butler saluted, turned and walked toward the door. His hand was on the knob when he was halted by Obode's voice.

"General, your report lacked one item."

Butler turned. "Oh?"

"Your women. What happened to them?"

"Dead," Butler said. "All of them."

"Good," Obode said. "Because if they lived they might speak. And if they spoke, it might be necessary for me to make an object lesson of you. We are not yet ready to defy the American government."

He meant it, Butler knew, which was why he had lied in the first place. Soon enough, Obode would be dead and the kidnapings could be blamed on him.

"Dead," Butler repeated the lie. "All dead."

"Don't take it so hard," Obode said. "When we are done with these accursed Loni, I will buy you a new whorehouse."

Obode smiled, then thought again of the thirteen soldiers dead at the hands of the American and the Oriental. "Better yet, Butler. Make that two companies of soldiers."

Princess Saffah came from the hut wiping her hands on a small cloth.

"She sleeps now," she told Remo.

"Good."

"She has been ill-treated. Her body has been used badly."

"I know."

"Who?" Saffah asked.

"General Obode."

Saffah spat on the ground. "The Hausa swine. I am glad that you and Little Father are here because soon we will be free of this evil yoke."

"How?" Remo asked. "We sit up here in the mountains. He sits down there in his capital. When are the twain going to meet?"

"Ask the Little Father. He carries in him the seed of all knowledge." She heard a slight moan behind her from inside the hut and without another word, turned and went inside to minister to her patient.

Remo walked off through the village. Chiun was not in his hut, which was built against the protection of a large stone formation, but Remo found him in the square in the center of the encampment.

Chiun wore a blue robe which Remo recognized as ceremonial, and the old man watched as Loni tribesmen stacked wood and twigs into a pit. The pit which had been dug that morning was twenty feet long and five feet wide. Its one-foot depth had been filled to the brim with wood, but in between the branches and twigs, Remo could see that the pit was filled with smooth white stones, the size of goose eggs.

As he watched, one of the tribesmen set the wood in the pit afire and the flames quickly spread until the entire pit was ablaze.

Chiun watched for a few moments, then said: "Adequate. But remember to keep the fire fed. It must not be allowed to dwindle."

He turned to Remo and waited for him to speak.

"Chiun, I've got to talk to you."

"I am writing my remembrances? I am watching my beautiful stories? Speak."

"The legend of the Loni," Remo said. "Does it say I get the shot at the baddie?"

"It says the man from the West who once died will grind into dust the man who would enslave the Loni. Is that an accurate English translation of what you have said?"

"All right," Remo said. "I just wanted to make it clear between us that I get the shot at Obode."

"Why is it so important to you now?" Chiun said. "After all, the House of Sinanju owes this debt. Not you."

"It's important to me because I want Obode. You didn't see what he did to those girls. He's mine, Chuin. I kill him."

"And what makes you think the legend has anything to do with your General Obode?" Chiun asked, and walked slowly away. Remo knew it would be useless to follow and ask just what he meant by that last statement; Chiun would speak only when the urge to speak came upon him.

Remo looked back toward the pit of fire. The dried wood had already passed the peak of its blaze and now the flames were lowering. The Loni tribesmen were busy feeding more wood into the fire, and over the sound they made, Remo could hear the stones in the pit cracking and splitting from the intense heat. An errant puff of wind blew across the pit toward Remo and the surge of heat sucked the breath from his lungs.

His inspection was interrupted by a shout from the hill that loomed over the small village. Remo turned and looked up.

"Tembo, tembo, tembo, tembo," the guard kept shouting. He was hollering and pointing out across the tree-speckled flatlands in the direction of the capital city of Busati.

Remo moved toward the edge of the plateau, hopped up onto a rock and looked in the direction the guard was pointing.

A big dust trail moved, perhaps ten miles away, across the plain. He forced his eyes to work harder.

Then he could pick out figures. There were jeeps with soldiers in them, and keeping up with the slowly moving vehicles were three elephants, soldiers on their backs, moving along in the stiff-legged elephant gait.

Remo sensed someone at his side. He looked down, saw Princess Saffah and extended a hand to help her up onto the stone. The guard was still shouting, "Tembo, tembo."

"What's he getting all worked up for?" Remo said.

"*Tembo* means elephant. In the Loni religion, they are considered animals of the devil."

"No sweat," Remo said. "A peanut or two, and keep the mice away."

"The Loni long ago sought a meaning for good and evil in the world," Saffah said. "Because it was so long ago and they had not yet science, they thought that animals embodied not only the good in the world but the bad. And because there was so much bad, they decided that only *tembo*—the elephant—was large enough to hold all that evil. He is a feared beast among the Loni. I did not believe Obode was smart enough to think himself of bringing elephants."

"This is Obode?" said Remo, suddenly interested.

"It can be no one else. The time draws near. Little Father has begun the fire of purification."

"Well, don't expect too much from the Little Father," Remo said. "Obode belongs to me."

"It shall be as Little Father wishes," Saffah said.

She hopped down and walked away and behind her back, Remo mumbled to himself, "As Little Father wishes. No, Little Father—Yes, Little Father—in your hat, Little Father. Obode's mine."

And then, he thought, his job would be over. Get the girl back to America; report to Smith what had happened, that the missing Lippincott was dead; and then forget this whole God-forsaken country.

CHAPTER FOURTEEN

Obode and his soldiers camped at the base of the hills in which the Loni camp sat, and throughout the day, tension built in the small mountainside village.

Remo sat with Chiun in his hut, trying to make conversation.

"These people got about as much backbone as a worm," he said.

Chiun hummed, his eyes fixed intently on the fire pit which shimmered heat and smoke at the other end of the village square.

"The men are wetting their pants just because Obode's got a couple of elephants. They're all ready to run away."

Chiun stared and hummed softly to himself but said nothing.

"I don't know how the House of Sinanju ever got into such a crap deal, taking care of these Loni. They're not worth it."

Chiun did not speak, and exasperatedly Remo said, "And another thing, I don't like this business about the fire ritual. I'm not letting you take any crazy chances of getting hurt."

Slowly, Chiun turned and confronted Remo. "There

is a proverb of the Loni," he said. *"Jogoo likiwika lisiwike, kutakucha."*

"Which means?"

"Whether the cock crows or not, it will dawn."

"In other words, whether I like it or not, you're going to do what you're going to do?"

"How quickly you learn," Chiun said and smilingly turned away to stare again at the fire.

Remo left the hut and wandered the village. All he heard, everywhere he went, was *"tembo, tembo, tembo."* The entire population was in a snit about a couple of elephants. Worry instead about Obode's soldiers and their guns. Pfooey. The Loni weren't worth saving.

He was annoyed and only later realized that he might be taking out his anger at Obode in annoyance against the Loni. The more he thought about it, the surer he was, and late that night, stripped naked, Remo slipped past the guards and out of the village. It was well after midnight when he returned. He moved silently, unseen, past the guards who capped the nearby rocks, stepped into his hut and immediately sensed the presence of someone else there.

His eyes scanned the bare hut and then saw the outline of a form on the raised grass mat which served as his bed.

He moved closer and the form turned. In the faint flicker from the flames in the ceremonial pit, he could make out Princess Saffah.

"You have been away," she said.

"I got tired of hearing everybody yelling *tembo.* I decided to do something about it."

"Good," she said. "You are a brave man." She lifted her hands toward him and he could feel and see the warmth of her smile. "Come to me, Remo," she said.

Remo lay down alongside her on the mat and she wrapped her arms around him. "When the sun is high tomorrow, you face your challenge," she said. "I want you now."

"Why now? Why not later?"

"What we have between us, Remo, may not survive a later. I have this feeling that all may be changed after tomorrow."

"You think I might lose?" Remo asked. Along the length of his warm flushed body, he felt the black coolness of her ebony skin.

"One can always lose, Remo," she said. "So one must take victories where one can. This now will be our victory. And then, no matter what happens on the morrow, we will always have this victory to remember."

"To victory," Remo said.

"To us," Saffah said, and with surprisingly strong arms moved Remo over her. "I was conceived a Loni and born a princess. Now make me a woman."

She placed Remo's hands on her breasts. "God made you a woman," he said.

"No. God made me a female. Only a man can make me a woman. Only you, Remo. Only this way."

And Remo did go into her and did know her and it could be truly written that on that hour she did become a well-made woman. And when both had done and the first rays of the sun were beginning to pink the sky, they slept, side by side, man and woman, God's team, by God's design.

And while they slept, General Obode arose.

It was barely dawn when he pushed aside the flaps of

his umbrella tent and, scratching his stomach, walked out into the pre-sun mist and did not like it at all.

His sergeant major's eyes scanned the camp quickly. The campfire had burned out. The guards who had been posted at the corners of the small campsite were not at their stations. There was too much stillness in the camp. Things bring stillnesses, the wrong things. There was sleep on duty and that was one kind of stillness but that was not this kind. And there was death, and this was that kind of stillness, which hung heavy in the air like a mist.

Obode stepped forward and with his toe kicked the ashes of the campfire. Not even an ember remained, not even a glow. Farther from his tent now, he looked around the camp. Next to him was General Butler's tent, its flaps still closed. All over the clearing lay the sleeping bags of the soldiers who had accompanied them, but the bags were empty.

He heard a sound ahead of him and looked up. The elephants had been chained to scrub trees up ahead, and they were hidden from his view by bushes. Despite his feeling of foreboding, Obode smiled. The elephants had been a good idea; the Loni fear of them was strong and traditional.

They must have seen them marching with Obode's soldiers and that must have terrified them. Today, Obode and his soldiers would storm the main Loni camp, and the Loni would look upon the slaughter that followed as inevitable, resign themselves to it as a historical fact. It had been a good idea. The great conquerors had used elephants. Hannibal and . . . Well, Hannibal anyway, thought Obode. Hannibal and Obode. It was enough to make a case.

The invincible elephant; the sign of the conqueror.

He thought for a moment to wake up Butler, but decided to let him sleep. This was a military matter for a military man, not a football player no matter how brave or loyal he was. He pushed his way through the bushes. Up ahead, forty yards away, he saw the vague gray forms of the elephants but there was something wrong with that too. Their outlines seemed somehow blunt and muted. And what was that before them on the ground? Slowly now, apprehensively, Obode moved forward through the thinning brush. Thirty yards now. Then twenty. And then he saw things clearly and his fingers rose to his lips in the Moslem supplication of mercy.

The elephants' outlines had been softened because their tusks were gone.

Like a moth pursuing a flame, despite himself, he went closer. The tusks of the three elephants had been hacked off near their bases. Only stumps of ivory remained, broken, chipped, craggy, like a memorable bad teeth that demanded the ministrations of tongue.

And the lumps on the ground. They were his men, his soldiers, and he did not have to look hard to be sure they were dead. Bodies lay there twisted, limbs askew, and through the chests of six of them, impaling them, spiking them to the ground were the six elephant tusks.

Obode, horrified, moved yet closer, impelled by some instinct of duty, some disremembered tradition that told the sergeant major he must be sure of his facts to be able to give a thorough report to the commander.

On the ground near the foot of one of the soldiers, he saw a piece of paper. He picked it up and looked at it.

It was a note penciled on the back of a printed military order that must have come from one of the soldiers:

The note read:

"Obode.

"I wait for you in the village of the Loni."

That was all. No name. No signature.

Obode looked around him. There had been two companies of soldiers here. Some must still be around, because these corpses sure weren't two companies worth.

"Sergeant," he bellowed. The sound of his voice rolled across the fields, across the land. He could almost hear it grow weaker as it traveled, unanswered, across the miles of Busati plain.

"Lieutenant," he shouted. It was as if he were shouting into a bottomless well in which sound reverberated but did not echo.

There was no sound and no sign of his soldiers.

Two whole companies?

Obode looked at the note in his hand again, thought deeply for a full ten seconds, dropped the paper, turned and ran. "Butler," he shouted as he neared the other tent. "Butler."

General William Forsythe Butler came from the tent, sleepy, rubbing his heavied eyes. "Yes, Mr. President?"

"Come on, man, we getting out of here."

Butler shook his head, trying to get a grasp on the morning's events. Obode flew past him into Obode's own tent. Butler looked around the camp. Nothing really unusual there. Except . . . except there weren't any soldiers to be seen. He followed Obode into his tent.

Obode was wrestling his white shirt on.

"What's wrong, Mr. President?" Butler asked.

"I'll tell you what's wrong. We leaving this place."

"Where are the guards?"

"The guards are dead or deserted. All of them," Obode said. "And the elephants. Their ivory been removed. We leaving. We leaving now 'cause I ain't gonna have nothing to do with nobody who can kill my soldiers and cripple my elephants in the night, without a sound, without a trace. Man, we getting out of here."

Obode brushed past Butler before his subordinate had a chance to speak. When Butler got back outside, the sun was beginning its climb into the sky and Obode was behind the wheel of one of the jeeps. He turned the ignition key to start position but nothing happened. He tried again, then with a curse jumped heavily down from the jeep and went to another vehicle.

That one would not start either.

Butler came to the jeep and opened the hood. The insides of the engine compartment had been destroyed. The battery had been broken in half, wires were ripped and wrenched apart, the distributor had been crushed into broken black powder and chips.

Butler inspected the other four jeeps in the clearing. They were all the same.

He shook his head at Obode, sitting disconsolately on the seat in the driver's seat of one of the vehicles.

"Sorry, General," Butler said, although he was not sure he was sorry at all. "If we go anywhere, we walk."

Obode looked up at Butler. "In this land we haven't a chance. Even the Loni could pick us off like flies."

"Then what do we do, Mr. President?"

Obode slammed a ham-sized fist down into the steering wheel of the jeep, cracking the wheel and sending the vehicle rocking back and forth on its wheels.

"Dammit," Obode shouted, "we do what armies should always do. We charge."

CHAPTER FIFTEEN

While Remo slept, Princess Saffah slipped out of his hut and went back to the hut where Hillary Butler slept.

Saffah could not recognize the feeling that gripped her on this day. All her life, she had waited for the legend to come true; now the men of the legend were here; soon the people of the Loni tribe would be restored to power; and yet, she felt a vague feeling of unease.

Legends were never simple. There were many ways for one to come true. Had they not, for instance, thought that Butler might be the Master of the legend? He had given up his former life in America to become the Loni's friend, so one might call him a dead man. And his returning to the Loni might fulfill the prophecy of the Loni children coming home. So she had thought, but that was wrong.

Might not other things be wrong? You are being a fool, child. What of Obode? Do you doubt that he is the evil man of the story? And that Remo must face him today? Yes, yes. And what of the Little Father? Doubt you that he will purify the Loni? No, no, but how? How?

Saffah ducked into the hut where the young American girl slept. She slid down smoothly onto her heels at the side of the small raised cot. The white girl breathed smoothly and evenly, and the faint trace of a smile played at the corners of her mouth. She would be well, Saffah knew, for one who could dream could live.

She put her ebony hand out and rested it on Hillary's pale white arm and looked down at the contrast. Hillary did not stir. Why was it so important, all this concern with color? Skin was skin, black or white or yellow as the Little Father's. What counted only was what was under the skin; the spirit, the heart, the soul. She looked at Hillary Butler and thought, might it not also be thus with tribes? Could hatred between Loni and Hausa end if they could only consider each other as people, good and bad, but each different?

She squeezed Hillary Butler's arm gently, reassuringly.

Chuin was up early and Remo found him at the pit of fire. The fire had been stoked and allowed to smolder during the night and now dry weeds and twigs were being thrown upon it.

As Chiun directed, four Loni tribesmen began to cover the unburned wood in the pit with leafy green branches of trees which dripped water, and sizzled and hissed on the white hot stones in the pit. Steam rose and smoke poured out from under the corners of the branches in lazy coils like drunken sated snakes.

"We going to have a cookout?" Remo asked. "Do you need a duck? I'll run to the store for hamburger rolls if you want."

"Need you go out of your way to appear gross?" Chiun asked. "For certainly, you need no assistance, no more than the duck needs help in quacking."

They were interrupted by a roar behind them. Along the trail, around the corner of the huts, striding into the village square came Obode and Butler, Obode leading the way, bellowing like a bull moose taunted by flies and gnats.

"Cowards and washwomen of the Loni tribe, General Obode is here. Come out, fly swatters and mosquito killers."

The village square was deserted as the few Loni men in it seemed to slip away. At one end of the square, near the fire pit, stood Remo and Chiun; at the other end, seventy five feet away, stood Butler and Obode. The four men stood looking at each other.

Out of a hut halfway between the two pairs came Princess Saffah. She stood black and tall, silent and majestic, wearing her almost-Grecian short robe, staring imperiously at Obode who continued to challenge the Loni men to combat, one at a time or all at once.

"Silence your mouth, braying beast," Saffah said finally.

"Who are you?" Obode shouted, after a moment's pause in which, Remo saw, he was stunned by Saffah's beauty.

"I am Saffah, first princess of the Loni Empire, and I order your silence."

"You order? *You* order? I am General Dada Obode, President of Busati, commander of all this land, and I am the one who orders."

"Perhaps in your brothels and in your pig sty of a capital, but here you can be silent. We are glad you came, General."

"When I am done," Obode said, "Perhaps you will not be so glad."

Saffah clapped her hands, three times, sharply. Slowly, obviously reluctantly, the Loni began to come from their huts, first women and children, and then men.

"We are glad you came nevertheless," she said smiling, as Loni men drew near Obode and Butler. "And you, Butler," she added, "you have done well to get the gross beast into our camp."

Butler gave a slight bow and Obode's head snapped toward him as if on a rubber band. Suddenly, so many things made sense. Butler was his traitor. Obode roared and lunged with both hands for Butler's throat. Butler was surprised by the attack and fell back before Obode's weight until Obode, at a signal from Saffah, was pulled away and restrained by six Loni tribesmen.

Chiun and Remo walked slowly down the length of the plaza toward Obode who still glared at Butler.

"Coward, traitor, Loni dog," Obode spat.

"Welcome to my people, fat pig," Butler said.

"You have not even the courage of the assassin," Obode said. "For you feared to take my life by yourself as you could have many times because I trusted you. Instead, you waited until you could deliver me into the hands of this flock of sheep."

"Discretion, General, discretion."

"Cowardice," Obode roared. "The armies I have known would have shot you like the dog you are."

Into the chaos, above the voices, rose the command of Chiun: "Silence. The Master of Sinanju says stop your tongues of women."

Obode turned toward Chiun who now stood directly in front of him and looked him over, as if he had just noticed him for the first time. The Basuti President towered over the aged Korean by a foot and a half. His weight was three times Chiun's.

"And you are the Master of the Loni legend?"

Chiun nodded.

Obode laughed, tipping his head back to offer his laughter to the sky. "Mosquito, stay out of Dada's way before I swat you."

Chiun folded his arms and stared at Obode. Behind Chiun, the square was now packed with people and they were hushed as if listening through thin walls to a family arguing next door.

Remo stood next to Chiun, peering coldly at Obode. Finally, the President's eyes met his.

Contemptuously, he asked: "And you? Another of the fortune-telling fairies?"

"No," Remo said. "I'm the chief elephant trainer and jeep repairman around here. Have a nice walk?"

Obode began to speak, then stopped, as if realizing for the first time that he was the prisoner of an overwhelmingly large number of enemies. Not as lowest recruit, not as British sergeant major, not as commander in chief of the Busati; but now, for the first time in his long career, he realized that death might be a real possibility.

"Kill him," Butler said. "Let us kill him and end this ancient curse on the Loni."

"Old ant," Obode said to Chiun, "since this is your party, I ask that when you kill me you do it like a man."

"Do you deserve the death of a man?"

"Yes," Obode said. "Because I have always given a man a man's death and I have tried to be fair. In my day, I wrestled regiments and no man feared to try to beat me because of my rank or station."

"Wrestling is very good for the teaching of humility," Chiun said. "It is the weakness of you Hausa that the most developed muscle in your body is your tongue. Come. I will teach you humility."

He walked back into the center of the open plaza, then turned to face Obode again. Remo came up alongside Chiun. "Chiun, he's mine. We agreed."

"Silence," Chiun ordered. "Do you think I would deprive you of your pleasure? It is written in the legend what you must do. You will do that; you will do no more."

He called to the Loni holding Obode:

"Release him."

Chiun wore his white *ge* the shin-length pants and white jacket known in America as a karate uniform. The jacket was tied with a white belt, which Remo recognized as an act of humility on Chiun's part. In the Westernization of the Oriental combat arts, the white belt was the lowest grading. Black belts were highest and there were various degrees of them. And then, beyond the black belt, beyond the knowledge of simple experts, there was the red belt, awarded to a handful of men of great courage, wisdom and distinction. The Master of Sinanju, foremost among the men of the world, was entitled to wear such a belt. Chiun instead had chosen beginner's white, and, as a beginner would, he wore it tied tightly around his waist.

He stood now in front of the fire pit where the continually dampened leaves and branches still steamed and smoldered, and beckoned to Obode.

"Come, one of the great mouth."

His arms free suddenly, Obode lunged forward, then slowed down and stopped. "This isn't right," he said to

Chiun. "I'm too big. How about your friend? I wrestle him."

"He has no more humility than you. The Master must teach you," Chiun said grandly. "Come. If you can."

CHAPTER SIXTEEN

Obode moved forward slowly, almost unwillingly, his heavy booted shoes kicking up little puffs of tan dust as he came.

He put a hand up in front of him, gesturing peace to Chiun. Chiun shook his head. "It is said the Hausa are brave and courageous. Are you the exception to that rule? Come. I will make the contest more even."

From under his sash, Chiun pulled a square of white silk, no more than eighteen inches on a side. He carefully placed it on the ground in front of him and stepped onto it, his body so light that his bare feet seemed not even to crinkle the cloth. "Come, loud one," he said.

Obode shrugged, a big heavy moving of his massive shoulders, and then he unbuttoned and stripped off his white uniform shirt. The sight of his shoulder muscle rippling black and sleek, almost purple under the hot African sun, drew a murmur from the crowd. And against him was arrayed only poor pathetic old Chiun, eighty years old, never having seen one hundred pounds, but standing, facing Obode, impassive, arms folded, his eyes like fiery hazel coals burning into the big man's face.

Obode tossed his shirt to the ground and Remo picked it up and moved past Obode to the rear of the square where General William Forsythe Butler stood. Obode kicked off his shoes; he wore no socks.

Remo turned to Butler. "Two bucks on the little guy, Willie," he said.

Butler refused to answer.

"I'll take it easy on you, old man."

Obode said that and lunged toward Chiun, his powerful arms spread wide. Chiun stood still, unmoving on his square of silk and let Obode engulf him in the black coils of muscles. Obode locked his hands behind Chiun's back, then arched his own back to lift Chiun off the ground, snapping as he would if lifting a heavy garbage pail. But Chiun's feet remained planted on the ground. Obode lurched again and almost fell backwards as Chiun remained rooted to the spot.

Then Chiun unfolded his arms, with delicate, slow majesty. He reached forward with both hands and touched two spots on the underside of Obode's arms. As if torched by electricity, Obode's arms released Chiun and flew wide apart.

He shook his head to clear it from the sudden jolt of nerve pain, then moved forward again toward Chiun, his left hand assorting air in front of him, seeking the classic wrestler's finger lock.

Chiun let Obode's hand approach his shoulder and then the President was flying through the air. Chiun had not seemed to move. His hands had not touched Obode, but the shift of Obode's weight was across Chiun's standing line of force, and Obode went somersaulting through the air to land with a thud on his back behind Chiun.

"Ooooof," he exploded.

Chiun turned slowly on the silken square until he was

facing the fallen Obode. Ripples of laughter went through the Loni men, standing around, as Obode raised himself to a kneeling position.

"Silence! Silence!" Chiun demanded. "Unless there is one among you who would take his place."

The noise subsided. Remo whispered to Butler, "Willie, you saved yourself two bucks." Privately, Remo was just a tinge surprised at how easily Chiun was handling Obode. Not that Obode represented any real danger. But Chiun was an assassin and how often had he told Remo that an assassin who could not, for some reason, enter combat prepared to kill his opponent was even more defenseless than the average man because the focus of his energy was dissipated and some of it must turn back upon himself. Yet, Chiun was obviously keeping Obode alive, and it did not seem to pose any special danger for Chiun. Oh well, Remo thought, that is why there is only one Master of Sinanju.

Obode was now on his feet. He turned toward Chiun, a questioning look on his face, and then lurched forward toward him. The old man stood in place, but when Obode neared him, Chiun shot out a silent swift hand. It planted itself near Obode's collarbone and Obode dropped as if he were a ball rolling off the end of a table. Except a ball bounces. The President of Busati didn't. He lay there in a dust-covered crumpled heap.

Chiun stepped back, retrieved his silk handkerchief, dusted it, folded it neatly and tucked it back in under his waistband.

"Take him," he said to no one in particular. "Tie him to that post."

Four Loni tribesmen dropped their spears and came out into the arena. They grabbed Obode by his hands and feet and tugged him, sliding along the ground, past the ceremonial fire pit which was still steaming and smoking, and to an eight-foot stake planted in the ground at the far end. Two of them propped the unconscious Obode up, while two more lifted his arms high and tied them with a rope through the large iron ring at the top of the eight-foot post.

Obode hung there, slowly regaining consciousness, hanging by his wrists. Chiun meanwhile had turned from him and looked to Saffah.

From the ground behind her, she lifted a golden brazier, shaped like a Japanese hibachi, and carried it by its handles toward Chiun. Heat waves shimmered off the bowl and the red glow of the burning coals it contained cast an aura around the golden dish. She placed it at the feet of Chiun.

Chiun looked down at the burning coals.

The silence of the moment was interrupted by a call from a sentry posted on the north side of the hill over the small encampment.

"Loni! Loni! Loni!" he called, obviously in great agitation. Remo turned and looked up toward him. He was waving an arm toward the hills to the north.

Remo moved to the edge of the camp and looked north. Coming up the hillsides, toward the encampment, were other natives, and Remo placed them instantly as Loni. The men were tall and lean and strong-looking; the women lithe and beautiful . . . two of them in particular.

The long chain of people was now only a hundred yards from the camp and the two women led the band of Loni men and women and children as if they were generals reviewing a parade. They were tall—black as night, their faces impassive and strong-boned, and Remo knew immediately these were the two younger sisters of Saffah, crown princess of the Loni.

Remo glanced back at Chiun. Chiun had sat in the center of the small square, his legs twisted into a full lotus, his fingertips in front of him in praying position. His eyes were closed and his face leaned forward toward the brazier of hot coals on the ground before him.

Remo looked at Chiun hard, but there was no way to tell what he was thinking or doing. The whole thing had confused Remo. Remo was to kill the evil man, but why had Chiun insisted upon playing with Obode first? Why not just give him to Remo? And what was this ritual purification by fire that Chuin was to do? And this nonsense about Chiun perhaps sacrificing his life? If it was anything dangerous, Remo would not let him do it. That was that case closed. No crap about it either.

And then the Loni were streaming into the village. There were hundreds of them, led by the two beautiful black women. As they came into camp, their impassiveness melted as they saw Saffah and each ran forward to be embraced by her.

It took fifteen minutes before the procession had ended; the square was now filled with all three existing Loni bands. Remo looked around. From what was once the greatest empire in all the history of Africa, this was left. Five hundred men, women and children. Hardly enough to fill a Newark tenement, much less create a new empire.

And still Chiun sat. The Loni looked at him silently as they crowded in around the village square, enclosing the pit of fire and an area the size of a large boxing ring.

They buzzed to themselves as they saw General Obode tied to the post at the far end of the pit of fire.

Obode was now awake, clearly wondering what was happening. His face darted from side to side, looking for an explanation, seeking a friendly face. He saw General William Forsythe Butler at the far end of the field and spat viciously onto the ground near his feet.

Inside a hut outside the square of people, Hillary Butler stirred. There was so much noise and it was so hot. But it was a nice hot; the kind of hot that makes your muscles work and your bones swing loose and easy. For the first time since she had entered the Loni village, Hillary Butler decided she would get up and walk outside and see what kind of place she was in.

But first she would nap just a few minutes more.

Saffah walked forward now to Chiun and stood in front of him, looking down at him across the heat waves rising from the brazier of coals.

"It is a great moment, Little Father. The legend has begun. The Loni children are home."

Chiun rose to his feet in one smooth fluid movement and opened his eyes. He turned and looked at the Loni men who continued to water down the leafy branches covering the fire pit, and nodded. They put down their containers of water and almost instantly the smoke from the pit grew heavier.

Chiun turned then and folded his hands in front of him.

"The legend is the truth," he intoned. "The Loni children are coming home.

"But wait! Are the Loni home? Are the Loni I see today the Loni that my ancestor served many years ago? Are these Loni, these Hausa-hating, elephant-fearing cowards who run like children in the night from noises they cannot see? Are these the Loni, whose bravest souls are their women?

"Are these the Loni that brought light and justice and knowledge to a dark world so many years ago?"

Chiun stopped and looked slowly, silently around the vast crowd, seeming to stop at each and every face, as if seeking an answer.

No one spoke and Chiun went on.

"The legend says that the Loni children will come home. And then the man who walks in the shoes of death must destroy the man who would enslave the Loni. And then the Master of Sinanju must purify the Loni people in the rites of fire.

"But this Master looks and wonders if these Loni can be redeemed."

Remo and Butler stood side by side, watching Chiun with equal intensity, thinking vastly different thoughts. He's going to renege, Remo thought. Did the House of Sinanju give refunds? Butler was exploring the depths of his satisfaction. Nothing had gone exactly as he had planned, but no matter. It seemed clear that before the day's events were over, Obode would be dead. The Loni would support the leadership of Butler; so would most of Obode's cabinet and most of the Army leaders. It would be a fine day for William Forsythe Butler, next President of Busati.

"Where is the nobility that once filled the hearts of the Loni people?" Chiun was saying.

"Gone like the fire goes," Chiun said, and as the crowd gasped, he reached his hands down into the golden brazier and brought out two handfuls of coals. Slowly, not even seeming to feel the heat, he scattered the coals around the ground. "Together, coals are a fire, but singly, they are but coals and soon die. It is thus with people; their greatness comes because each shares in the tradition of their greatness." He dropped again to his haunches, and began scattering with his hands the coals from the brazier.

Behind him, the leaves and twigs still smoldered, the heat waves rising from the pit like steam from a subway grating.

Inside the hut, Hillary Butler could no longer sleep. She got to her feet, happily surprised that she wore so sparkling clean a blue robe. She knew now that she was going to be all right. That evil house; the man on the ship; it was all behind her now. She would soon be home; she would be married as she had planned; somehow she knew that everything would be all right.

She moved toward the entrance to the hut, her steps weak and slightly shaky.

Outside the hut, Remo stood next to General Butler. "Willie," Remo said, putting his arm conspiratorially around the other man's shoulder, "you were a good one. But that was a good team you played for. Tell me something I always wanted to know. Did you guys shave the point spread? I remember, you guys were always like five-point favorites and you always wound up winning by three. You cost me a lot of bucks, Willie. I never could figure why you guys would shave. I mean, you were making the big dough already; it just wouldn't seem to be worth the risk. You know, it's not like you were slaves or anything, Willie."

Hillary Butler stepped out of the hut and blinked in the bright sunshine. Just ahead of her, she saw Remo and she smiled. He had been so nice. His arm was around that black man in the white uniform and they were talking.

"Get out of here, for Christ's sake, will you?" William Forsythe Butler said to Remo. He raised his right hand to Remo's shoulder and pushed. Something on his hand glinted in the sun. It was a ring. A gold ring. A gold ring formed in the links of a small chain.

Hillary Butler had seen that ring before. Just once, when the heavy black hand holding the chloroform pad had lowered over her face.

Hillary Butler screamed.

Remo turned, as silence descended over the entire village. The white girl stood there in the entrance to the hut, her mouth open, her finger slowly raising to point. Remo came to her side.

"Oh, Remo," she said. "You've got him."

"Got him? Oh yeah, right. Obode," Remo said. "He's tied up down there."

"No, no, not Obode. That one," she said, pointing to Butler. "He was the one who took me from my house. He kidnaped me."

"Him?" Remo said, pointing to Butler.

She nodded and shuddered.

"Old Willie?" Remo asked.

"That one," she said pointing.

Suddenly everything had come undone for William Forsythe Butler, but perhaps there was still a chance. He broke through the crowd, pulling the pistol from his holster, running toward Obode. He might yet manage it. Kill Obode, then say he took the girl under Obode's orders.

He raised the gun to fire. Then the gun was gone from his hand, thudding softly, sending up a little puff of dust where it hit the ground and Chiun stood alongside him.

Butler stopped in his tracks.

"You have done evil to the Loni people," Chiun said. "Did you hope someday to be king of this land? To one day enslave not only Hausa but Loni too?" Chiun's voice rose in pitch.

Butler slowly backed away from him. "You have disgraced the Loni people. You are not fit to live."

Butler turned to try to run, but there was no break in the crowd. He turned. Then Chiun turned his back on him and was walking away.

Remo moved out into the clearing.

"It was you, Willie?"

"Yes," Butler hissed, the Loni click in his throat chattering his anger. "I would repay in kind what the whites did to me. What they did to the Loni people."

"Sorry, Willie," Remo said, remembering the girls he had been forced to kill. "You were a good cornerback but you know how it is: you can't argue with a legend."

He moved toward Butler, who drew himself up to his full height. He was bigger than Remo, heavier, probably stronger. The white bastard had never been able to forget for one minute that he had been Willie Butler. All right. So be it. Now he would show him what Willie Butler could do if he had wanted to play the white man's game.

He crouched down and from deep in his throat growled at Remo: "Your ball, honkey."

"I'm going to flood your zone with receivers," Remo said. "That always confused you goons."

Remo began trotting toward Butler who went wide-legged into a tackling stance. When Remo was within reach, he sprang, leaving his feet, rolling on his side toward Remo. Remo skipped lightly over him and Butler quickly rolled up onto his feet.

"First and ten," Remo said.

He came back toward Butler who assumed the same stance, but this time as Remo drew near, Butler straightened up, leaped into the air and let fly a kick at Remo's face. Remo caught the heel of the foot in both hands and continued pushing it upward, tumbling Butler back over onto his back.

"Unsportsmanlike conduct, Willie. That'll cost you fifteen yards."

Butler got up again and charged now in a rage at Remo, who dodged away. "Tell me, Willie, what was it you were trying to prove? What'd you need the girls for?"

"How could you know? That accursed family . . . the Butlers, the Forsythes, the Lippincotts . . . they bought my family as slaves. I was collecting a debt."

"And you think that poor little girl over there had something to do with it?"

"Blood of blood," Butler grunted, as he wrapped his arms around Remo's waist. "The bad seed has to be uprooted, no matter how big it's grown." He slid off Remo to the ground as Remo skipped away.

"It's people like you, Willie, that give racism a bad name."

Butler had edged around, slowly facing Remo, moving in a circle. He widened the circle gradually until his back was against the line of Lonis who were quietly watching this contest, so unlike anything they had ever seen.

Without warning, Butler reached behind him, grabbed

a spear from one of the Loni men and jumped back into the squared arena.

"At last, your true colors come out," Remo said. "You're just another dirty player."

Butler moved toward him with the spear, holding it like a javelin, his hand on its middle, its weight poised over his right shoulder, ready to throw.

"Now you tell me something, white man. The legend says a dead man comes with the Master. How are you a dead man?"

"Sorry, Willie, it's true. I died ten years ago. Now you can worry about the legend."

"Well, dying didn't seem to take. So I think you ought to try it again."

Butler was only six feet from Remo now and he reared back with the spear and let it fly. Its point flew straight at Remo's chest and Remo collapsed backwards out of its way and as the spear passed over his head, Remo's hand flashed out and cracked the center of the shaft. The spear snapped in two, both halves clattering across the ground toward Chiun, who stood quietly watching.

Remo slowly regained his feet. "Sorry, Willie, you just lost the ball on downs."

And then Remo moved toward him with a leap.

"This one's for the Gipper," Remo said.

Butler rammed a forearm toward the bridge of Remo's nose but the arm struck only air and then Willie Butler felt a biting pain in his chest that turned to fire and the fire was flashing red and pure and it burned worse than all the fires he'd ever seen and in that last flash of flame, he thought back, and his mind said, it's me, Sis, it's Billie, I really can run fast because I know it, and someday I'm gonna be a big man and his sister was saying no tomming swamp nigger ever gonna amount to anything, but Sis, you were wrong, I was wrong, hate and violence isn't the way, it just doesn't work, but his sister didn't answer and suddenly Willie Butler didn't care anymore because he was dead.

Remo stood up and rolled Butler over with his foot so his face was buried in the dust.

"That's the biz, sweetheart," he said.

The Loni were still silently watching. Chiun moved toward Remo, put his hand on Remo's arm and said loudly: "Two parts of the legend are now completed."

He looked slowly around the circle of Loni, confused and staring, then at Obode who had regained his dignity and stood erect, his arms yanked high up over his head, determined to die like a British soldier.

"The evil in the world is not always Hausa evil," Chiun said. "The Loni curse has not been the Hausa, but the Loni people who have no heart. We must give you back your heart."

Chuin released Remo's arm and turned toward the fire pit. Almost as if by signal, the last of the water evaporated, and the pit went aflame with a searing whoosh that seemed to swallow the oxygen in the arena and that moved Obode back, cringing slightly.

From a bowl alongside the pit, Chiun took salt and began sprinkling it at the end of the pit, seemingly oblivious to the heat. While Chiun's ritual went on, Saffah and her two sisters moved forward behind Chiun.

The flames died quickly as the dried-out wood almost exploded into fire and Chiun motioned to the two Loni men who stood near the rear corners of the pit. Using long staves, they began to spread the fire, shaking the twigs and embers loose, and exposing through the fire the giant ostrich egg-sized rocks, now glistening white hot from their two-day baking.

Remo came up alongside Chiun.

"What the hell are you up to?" he demanded.

"One does not worry about the Master. One only observes and learns." Chiun looked at Remo, seemed to understand his concern and said, "No matter what happens you must promise not to interfere. No matter what."

"Chiun, I won't let you do anything foolish."

"You will do as I say. You will not interfere. My House's debt to the Loni has been a family disgrace. You dishonor me if you stop me from discharging that debt. Do nothing."

Remo searched Chiun's eyes for any weakness, any hint, but there was none.

"I don't like it," Remo said glumly, even as he started moving back.

"Your preferences are of little interest to my ancestors. They like what I do."

The entire pit had now been raked until it was an evil mix of white hot stones and red hot embers.

Chiun looked around him at the Loni people. "The Lonis must again be taught of bravery."

He nodded to Princess Saffah and her sisters and they slowly walked forward in a single line toward the pit. Remo stood alongside and watched them, a procession of three proud and beautiful women. He could understand why once this land had great kings and queens. Saffah and her sisters were royalty in any land in any day. Traditional royalty was a gift of governments or an accident of heritage, but real royalty came from the soul. The sisters had soul.

Saffah stepped into the ritual bed of salt Chiun had prepared, then folding her arms, without hesitation, she placed her right foot into the bed of hot coals and began to walk into the pit of fire. The Loni gasped. Remo stood stunned. Obode appeared in a state of shock.

But oblivious to all their feelings was Saffah, who was now walking, resolute step after resolute step, down the center line of the pit. Her feet kicked up little clouds of sparks and heat shimmered around her bare ankles. When she was halfway across, the next sister stepped through the salt pit and out into the coals. And a few moments later, the third sister followed.

Remo watched their faces carefully; not a sign of pain or concern showed. It was some kind of trick. Cheapie old Chiun had done some finangling with the fire. Unworthy, Remo decided. Definitely unworthy of a Master of Sinanju. He would have to tell him.

The three sisters now stood in a row near Obode at the far end of the fire pit.

"Your princesses have shown you that the Loni can still breed courage," Chiun said, "but that is not enough to purify you."

Chiun stepped his bare wrinkled yellow feet into the small salt bed and then he too stepped out into the field of flame and fire and heat.

As he walked, he intoned a chant softly to himself. *"Kufa tutakufa wote."* Remo had never heard it before but recognized it as part of the Loni tongue.

Carefully, yet decisively, Chiun walked straight along the length of the fire bed.

And then in the middle he stopped.

Good trick, Remo thought. A real show-stopper, Chiun.

Chiun stood there, feet not moving, arms folded, face impassive as ever, still mouthing his chant. *"Kufa tutakufa wote."*

"What's that mean?" Remo said to a Loni standing behind him.

"It means, As for dying, we shall all die."

The Loni watched Chiun and their small buzzings turned to silence as the seconds ticked on and Chiun stood still in the middle of the fiery pit, the heat waves rising around him, making his body seem to shimmer and shake even though he did not move.

Then a small wisp of smoke began to curl up the side of Chiun's leg. Remo could see that Chiun's shin-length white pants had singed at the bottom. A little speck turned brown, then black, then broadened, and now gave out thin trails of smoke. An orange dot appeared at the edge of one leg as the overheated fabric neared its flash point. A tiny lick of flame puffed up.

The Loni gasped. Remo took a step forward, then stopped, indecisive, not knowing what to do.

And over the gasping and the whispers roared the voice of General Obode.

"Will no one help that man?"

The roar was an anguished cry.

Yet no one moved.

"Help him," Obode demanded at the top of his voice.

Still no one moved.

With a bellow of rage and anger, Obode wrenched at the eight-foot post to which he was tied.

The force of his huge body tore the iron ring from its mounting and his hands came loose, still tied together with the ring now suspended on the rope connecting his wrists.

Chiun's *ge* was breaking into flame at the shins, at the waist.

Without hesitation, Obode raced forward the two steps separating him from the fire pit, seemed to pause momentarily, and then, barefooted, ran through the pit to the place Chiun stood. Each step he took, he screamed. Yet he ran on. When he reached Chiun, he scooped with both hands together and lifted Chiun in his giant arms like a baby, then ran the short distance across the pit to exit at the side. He put Chiun down gently and with his hands began to beat out the flames of Chiun's uniform. Only when they were out, did he roll onto his back and begin to try wiping away the glowing bits of wood and rock that still stuck to his burned-black feet. He was still screaming in pain.

The Loni watched quietly as Chiun sat unconcerned and Obode ministered to his feet.

And then, a full-throated cheer went up from the watching crowd. Hands clapped in the peculiar unrhythmic African manner. Women shouted approval. Children whistled. The Loni princesses left their places and came running toward Obode and Chiun. Saffah snapped her fingers and shouted some words. In a seeming split second, women were back with leaves and buckets that appeared filled with mud and Saffah began making a poultice for Obode's feet.

Remo came over and as he moved in front of Chiun, he saw with astonishment that Chiun's feet were unmarked and so were his legs and hands. His uniform was singed and scorched, in places crisped away into hard flecks of black charcoal, but Chiun was unhurt.

As Remo stood there, Chiun moved to his feet and stood over the figures of the three princesses ministering to General Obode.

"People of the Loni, hear me now and hear me well because I have traveled many miles to bring you these words." He waved a hand toward Obode, writhing on the ground in pain.

"You have learned through this man today that the Hausa may have courage. It is the beginning of wisdom. You have applauded his courage, and that is the beginning of self-worth. The Loni did not lose an empire because of the Hausa. They lost it because they were not fit to hold it. Today, your people have regained their fitness. The legend has been redeemed. The debt of the House of Sinanju has been paid."

One voice piped out of the crowd. "But our return to power. What of that?" Several voices mumbled in concert with him.

Chiun raised his hands for silence. "No man bestows power, not even the Master of Sinanju. Power is earned by deeds and works. The President of the Hausa has learned something today. He has learned that the Loni no longer hate him because he is a Hausa. They have hated him because he has been unjust. Today he is going to become a great leader because he will now bring the Loni into the palaces of government to build again a great land. The Loni will not be sergeants and servants; they will be generals and counselors." Chiun looked down at Obode whose eyes met his. They locked momentarily and Obode nodded in agreement, then looked away, back at the head of Princess Saffah who still ministered to his burned feet, her long black silken hair splashing about his blistering ankles.

"To keep this new power, the Loni must be worthy," Chiun said. "And then soon there may be a new race of kings in this land. With the bravery of the Hausa, with the beauty and wisdom of the Loni."

He looked now at Saffah. She looked at him and then, with tenderness, at Obode, then nodded to Chiun. She smiled and reached out her hand and placed it on Obode's shoulder.

"People of the Loni, the legend is done. You may tell your children you saw the Master. You may tell them also he will return if ever man's hand is set unfairly against you people whom I protect."

With those words, Chiun dropped his hands and walked toward his hut. He picked Hillary Butler from the crowd, took her arm and led her inside with him.

Remo followed and found Chiun sitting on his prayer mat. Hillary Butler sat on the floor near him, just watching.

Chiun looked up, saw Remo, and said: "Where were you when I needed you?"

"You told me not to interfere."

"Ah yes, but would a worthy son have listened? No. He would have said, ah, that is my father, he is in danger, nothing must stop me from saving him. That is what a loyal son would have said. It is the difference between good breeding and being something the cat dragged in."

"Well, it didn't really matter anyway. It was just a trick. Nobody stands on hot coals."

"Come," Chiun suggested. "We will go out and walk the fire together. It is done often in the civilized sections of the world," meaning, Remo knew, the part of the world Chiun came from. "Japanese do it. Even some Chinamen."

"But how?" Remo said.

"Because they are at peace with themselves," Chiun said triumphantly. "They think of their souls instead of their stomachs. Of course to do that one must first have a soul."

"Bicker, bicker, bicker," Remo said. "It was still a trick."

"The stupid never learn; the blind never see," Chiun said and would say no more.

Remo turned to Hillary Butler. "We'll get you started on your way home tonight."

She nodded. "I want . . . well, I want to thank you. I don't really understand all this, but maybe . . . well, anyway thank you."

Remo raised a hand. "Think nothing of it."

Chiun said, "You may be grateful. The Master has done what he had to do. This one . . . well, he did the best he could."

Later, as they prepared to leave, Remo stood near the graying fire pit, and picked up a small chip of wood from the ground. He flipped it out into the pit of coals. The chip of wood hit, seemed to break up the steady pattern of heat waves for a split second, then flared into flame.

Remo shook his head. He turned, and saw Chiun standing there, smirking.

"There is still time for you to learn the fire walk."

"Try me next week," Remo said.

Remo, Chiun and Hillary Butler left the Loni camp that night with a hundred-man Loni escort, fourteen of them with no other responsibility but to carry Chiun's luggage.

Saffah and Obode bade them good-bye, then Saffah took Remo to one side.

"Good-bye, Remo," she said. She began to say something else, stopped herself, said a word that sounded to Remo like *"nina-upenda"* and walked quickly away from him.

On the trail down the mountainside, Chiun said more to himself than to Remo, "I am glad we did not have to kill Obode."

Remo glanced at him, suspiciously. "Why?"

"Hmmm?" Chiun said. "Oh, there is no reason."

"There is a reason for everything you say," Remo said. "Why are you glad we didn't have to kill Obode?"

"Because the chief of the Hausa is to be protected."

"Who says? Why?" Remo demanded.

Chiun was silent.

"Two-faced sonuvabitch. I'm going to get Smith to get the Washington pollsters to take the soap operas off again."

Chiun considered this for a moment. "There is no need for you to punish an old man."

"Then talk. Why was Obode to be protected?"

"Because when my ancestor many years ago left the Loni and they were overthrown . . ." Chiun paused.

"Get on with it."

"He left to go work for the Hausa," Chiun said. "For more money," he explained brightly.

"Well, I'll be. Talk about double-dealers," Remo said. "Has any Master ever played anything straight?"

"You know not the meaning of such words," Chuin answered.

"Yeah? Well, try this. *Nina-upenda,"* he said, repeating the Loni word that Saffah had spoken to him.

"Thank you," Chiun said and Remo had to find out later from one of their guards that the word meant "I love you."

It made him feel good all over.